A Donut
for Your
Thoughts

A Donut
for Your
Thoughts

Coco Simon

Simon Spotlight

New York London Toronto Sydney New Delhi

SIMON SPOTLIGHT
An imprint of Simon & Schuster Children's Publishing Division
1230 Avenue of the Americas, New York, New York 10020
This Simon Spotlight paperback edition August 2020
Copyright © 2020 by Simon & Schuster, Inc.
All rights reserved, including the right of reproduction in whole or in part in any form.
SIMON SPOTLIGHT and colophon are registered trademarks of Simon & Schuster, Inc.
Text by Samantha Thornhill
For information about special discounts for bulk purchases, please contact Simon & Schuster Special Sales at 1-866-506-1949 or business@simonandschuster.com.
Designed by Ciara Gay
The text of this book was set in Bembo Std.
Manufactured in the United States of America 0720 OFF
10 9 8 7 6 5 4 3 2 1
ISBN 978-1-5344-7373-7 (hc)
ISBN 978-1-5344-7372-0 (pbk)
ISBN 978-1-5344-7374-4 (eBook)
Library of Congress Catalog Card Number 2020940546

Chapter One
The Dream Team

"Casey Peters to the rescue! Yasss!"

I hung up the phone and tossed it onto the bed, pumped the music up loud, and danced around my room.

It was Monday after school and I had nothing planned, so I was excited to get called in to work with my BFF, Lindsay Cooper, at her family's restaurant, which also happens to sell the most delicious donuts ever made.

Back in the day, Lindsay's grandparents, Grandpa and Nans Cooper, opened the Park View Table, which is now a booming family business in Bellgrove, Missouri. True to its name, it sits right across the street from and has a dashing view of, you guessed it, the park!

Between Nans's finesse in the kitchen and Grandpa's tight ship on the floor, the Park is the only restaurant in town worth talking about, with its legit menu and flawless service.

Nans initially started the Donut Dreams counter in the Park to stack enough dough (so to speak!) to send Lindsay's dad, their oldest child, to the university of his dreams. Unlike his brother and sister, who stayed close to home, Mike Cooper ended up going away to school in Chicago.

There, he fell in love with Lindsay's mom, Amy, and traveled to Europe with her. Amazingly, out of all the places they could have chosen to live in this whole wide world, they came right back to Bellgrove to put down roots and have kids—Lindsay and her younger brother, Skylar, aka. Sky.

Lindsay's dad took over Donut Dreams, and Lindsay's mom became an art teacher at Bellgrove Middle School until she passed away a few years ago.

My mom says it was Amy Cooper's choice to settle here instead of some big city or foreign land. Mom knows this because my mom and Lindsay's mom were the original BFFs! They even ended up having Lindsay and me at the same time, literally. Lindsay and I first mingled cries in the hospital, since we were born one day apart. Our oldest photo together is with our moms in the hospital nursery. And the rest is history.

My mom loves to tell me how Lindsay and I used to stare at each other in the hospital and smile and coo to each other. She just assumed we were just friendly babies, but we never did that with anyone else.

Then a few weeks after we both were home with our families, my mom brought me over to Lindsay's house for a visit. She says the minute we saw each other again, we reached out for each other and cooed and giggled and laughed. True BFFs from the start!

I guess Lindsay's mom actually preferred the charmed small-town life that Lindsay and others hope to escape. I totally understand why Lindsay wants out—going to school with the same kids since kindergarten, everyone is always in your business, that sort of thing.

But small-town life also has its perks. Not only delectable donuts, but also this feeling of safety and being known by everyone you see.

The truth is, Donut Dreams is more than just a pretty name for a donut spot. People patiently wait in line here just to sink their teeth into the pillowy sweetness of a banana cream or elderberry jelly donut.

Without Nans's bright idea, Lindsay's parents would never have met in Chicago, which means my best friend wouldn't be my best friend, because Lindsay wouldn't even be a thing in my life.

And where, oh where, would I be without Lindsay Cooper?

I feel honored to be the only non-family member who works at the Park on days like today, when one of Lindsay's cousins has a cold or a big exam.

All of Lindsay's aunts, uncles, and cousins are employees at the restaurant. The only family member of hers who isn't recruited to work at the restaurant is her brother Skylar, aka. Sky, who's nine.

I pranced over to my dresser and pulled out my yellow Donut Dreams T-shirt, the back of which read THE DREAM TEAM. Thankfully, I keep my room pretty neat—except for the closet and under the bed, that is—so I wasn't tripping over stuff looking for my stretchy jeans when my mom popped into my room carrying a load of clean laundry.

My mom is the assistant principal of Bellgrove Middle School, where I just started going this year.

A Donut for Your Thoughts

Ever since she got her back-to-school hairdo, I admired how her reddish-brown ringlets framed her perfect round face.

"Casey, it sounds like New Year's Eve in here!" she was shouting. "What's going on?"

I lowered the music. "They need my help at Donut Dreams today," I said. "Is it okay if I work for a few hours, Mom? Pleeeease?"

I already knew what the answer would be. As long as I ace my schoolwork and keep my room somewhat tidy, any opportunity I have to be responsible is all right with Laurie Peters.

"I hope you'll always be this enthusiastic about work," Mom said with a laugh. "Go ahead and make some dollars . . . not eat empty calories!"

Mom knows me to a T. Lindsay and I always manage to sneak in a donut or two when no one's looking.

"Yes!" I cheered, my mouth already watering.

Mom left my room, and I went back to zipping around in search of my comfiest jeans to wear (why is it that even though my room is pretty neat, I can never find what I want to wear when I want to wear it?).

I finally found them and paired them with the bright Donut Dreams shirt that makes me feel like a superhero whenever I slip it over my head.

Even though I see Lindsay all the time, it was still exciting to work with my BFF. Plus, every time I was at Donut Dreams, I felt inspired.

Let's just say, there's something dreamy about spending time in a place so creative and colorful!

Chapter Two
First Crush?

"Casey, are you ready?" Mom called from downstairs minutes later.

The car keys jingled as she lifted them from the hook by the front door.

I hurriedly swept up my hair into a messy bun, slipped my phone into my back pocket, and galloped down the stairs, grinning from ear to ear.

On the way to the Park, my thoughts drifted to Matt Machado. Matt is a friend I made at sleepaway camp this summer. Ever since I came home from camp, he's never been too far from my mind.

Before meeting him, I can't say I was really into boys. I'm still not, but Matt's different. He isn't lame like the other boys at camp or the Bellgrove boys I've been ignoring since kindergarten. We actually have real stuff in common, not just liking the same candy or music or whatever.

For instance, we're both biracial, except his mom's black and his dad's white, and my parents are the opposite. Before meeting Matt, the only other biracial person I knew was my older sister, Gabby, but she doesn't count.

I have friends at camp that I've known from years of going there, but Matt was new this summer and didn't know anybody until we met at orientation on the first day, during one of those corny icebreaker activities.

We became camp BFFs, which made some of my other camp friends jealous, because just like with Lindsay, once we clicked, I wanted to spend every spare moment with Matt.

We would find each other during breakfast and eat together before jetting off to our different activities. Then we'd loop back in for lunch before kayaking together on the lake and then we'd have dinner. Sometimes we'd end our days at the campfire. At camp we were each other's worlds.

After being two peas in a pod all summer, it was

strange not being in each other's business all day, every day.

We've texted back and forth a few times, but there's no rhythm to it. And whenever he does text back, sometimes days later, it's usually a one-word response.

Ugh. Back to reality, I guess. Whatever.

Since I was in such a good mood and everything, I thought about texting him something funny to help him remember the jokes we shared . . . in case he forgot.

Matt thought I was hilarious and got 95 percent of my jokes. I hadn't realized I could have such a wicked sense of humor with anyone else besides Lindsay.

I stared into my phone and thought about what to text.

I must say, it's harder to plan on being funny than to just be funny naturally, in the moment. I couldn't think of anything to say and lost track of time.

I must have been staring into the distance, not saying anything, for too long because Mom took notice.

"With Lindsay hard at work, I wonder who else could have you so deep thought," Mom said.

She peeled her eyes from the road for an instant to glance down at the blinking cursor on my phone.

Mom never misses a beat, especially when it comes to me. She knows Lindsay is the only person that I text 24/7, and there's a no-texting rule for all workers at the Park.

I hadn't breathed Matt's name to anyone besides Lindsay. The only reason Mom would know that Matt existed was if she noticed his picture in my room on the bulletin board, but she never asked me anything about him.

"Nobody special," I answered, my face warming.

I fired off some silly cat meme to Matt and put my phone away.

But oh, Matt was special. He was funny, smart, mysterious, and certifiable eye candy.

I never had a reason to talk to my mom about a boy before, and even now, I wasn't sure if there was anything to talk about besides our kayaking and campfire coziness.

And that wasn't something to bring up to your assistant principal mom . . . or was it?

Thankfully, we arrived at the restaurant before Mom could dig any deeper.

A Donut for Your Thoughts

"Have a good afternoon working hard," Mom said, beaming with pride.

"Thanks, Mom. And I'll try to save room for dinner after I've sampled every kind of donut in the case!"

I let out a wicked laugh, leaped out of the car, and shut the door before she could open her mouth to protest.

Chapter Three
Picture Perfect

"There she is!" said Lindsay's grandfather when he spotted me breezing through the doors of the Park.

I made a beeline for the podium near the entrance, where Grandpa Coop greets his hungry customers and oversees the floor to make sure everything is sanitary and moves smoothly. When I got to him, I gave him a big hug.

"How's my honorary grandchild?" he asked.

I adore everything about Lindsay's grandfather, like he's my own. I love how he makes such intense eye contact with every person he speaks to, and how he makes it a point to greet everyone who enters the restaurant. He has this way of making everyone feel special and seen. I also love his crinkly eyes and how the lines in his face tell a story of who he is—someone who likes to laugh as hard as he likes to work.

I even love how he manages the Park with his "iron fist, sunny glove" style. Along with the delicious food, the restaurant's level of friendly professionalism is key to its success. Grandpa Coop is strict about certain things—okay, well, everything. Counter crumbs and sauce smears make him cranky, and his radar for fake smiles from his staff is crazy accurate.

He's no-nonsense about the rules, but never unpleasant. I don't know how he does it. Even when he throws us his signature side-eye for having our phone in hand at work, or reminds us to wipe a teeny smudge we missed off the glass display, no one ever feels like they're being bossed around.

"Thank you for coming on such short notice to save the day," he cheered.

Grandpa Coop always has this way of making me feel like a vital part of the restaurant.

"Now go rescue your other half behind the donut counter!" he said.

Clearly, my BFF needed some rescuing, because she was swamped.

After going into the back to wash my hands,

clock in, put on an apron, and glance at the inventory, I raced over to the Donut Dreams counter.

Lindsay looked a bit overwhelmed as she struggled to serve the first wave of the elementary school crowd, three squealing Girl Scouts. Her gloved hand hovered over a different donut each time the girls changed their minds. By the look on Lindsay's face, this had been going on for some time.

"The pink one with sprinkles . . . no, wait. The chocolate one. No, wait! Maybe the glazed. Ooh, I don't know which one I want!" said one of the girls.

Lindsay stood there silently, but knowing her, especially after a full day at school, she was probably cranky and losing her patience.

I put on my best smile and swooped in to join her behind the counter.

"Can I make a suggestion?" I asked. "How about lemon cream? It's like eating two kinds of donuts with every bite. It's so yummy—sweet and tangy at the same time."

"Ooh, that sounds . . . dreamy!" one girl said, making the others giggle. "Give me that one!"

"Make it two! Make it three!" the others chimed in, raising their hands.

A Donut for Your Thoughts

Lindsay smiled at me gratefully as she put the donuts in the bag I opened for her and rang up their order. After the girls left with their bag of donuts, she high-fived me.

"You're a lifesaver!" Lindsay said. "What made you suggest the lemon cream?"

I shrugged.

"I looked at the inventory and noticed we had a lot of lemon donuts. Those girls obviously didn't know what they wanted, so I just gave them a push in the lemon donut direction," I said.

"Genius!" Lindsay said. "They were cute, but a couple more minutes and I would have paid for their donuts and pushed them in the 'get out now' direction!"

I laughed at the thought of Lindsay doing such a thing and tried to imagine Grandpa Coop's stern expression lasting for more than ten seconds. It made me wonder if he would ever fire one of his grandchildren for getting cranky with a customer.

I almost jumped when my phone buzzed in my back pocket, which, oops, was actually supposed to be stowed under the counter during my shift. It was just a text alert, but my heart was racing.

I looked around to make sure that Grandpa Coop's

eagle eyes weren't focused in my direction and took a quick peek.

Sigh. My heart slowed in its tracks. It was just my mom, trying to be funny.

You'll want to keep your stomach empty for what's cooking. Now put your phone under that counter and get back to work!

That's my mom, all right. She always has to have the last word.

I sighed again, but a little part of me wondered what yummy thing Mom was making for dinner as I put my phone away.

"Don't worry, he didn't see you," Lindsay told me, eyeing Grandpa Coop.

One thing I love about our friendship is how we always have each other's backs.

"Thanks," I said.

I put my phone next to hers. When I looked up again, Lindsay was studying me.

"Whoever you're texting with must be mighty

important to risk a scolding from Grandpa," she said with a giggle. "And I'm right here! Who could be more important than me?"

"No one is more important than you," I assured her. "It's just . . . well . . ."

"Come on . . . spit it out," Lindsay said.

She stared at me while I busied myself wiping the already spotless display glass.

Lindsay knows all too well how embarrassed I get by my own feelings—big or small—and I can't stand to be embarrassed.

Maybe that's why it's so difficult for me to say how I really feel. Something I like about Lindsay's family is how open and messy they are with each other sometimes, but it's clear that the love is always there.

"Before I got here I sent my friend Matt a text, and I was kind of hoping this was him texting back. But it wasn't," I explained.

Okay, that wasn't so bad.

"Ohhhh, I see," Lindsay said.

She continued to look at me carefully. "So what's the deal with you guys?"

"There is no 'deal,'" I said.

I could feel the temperature of my cheeks shoot up a few degrees.

"Uh-huh," she said, clearly not convinced.

"We're just good friends, and I sent him something I thought he'd think was funny, and I'm just . . ." I trailed off.

"Wondering if he thought it was funny?" Lindsay finished my sentence for me.

"Yes," I said. "That's all."

But what I didn't say was that every time I get a text, my heart starts pounding fast until I see who sent it. And when it's not him, I start to feel really sad and I'm not even sure why, because he's not even my boyfriend.

Why I couldn't say this to Lindsay, I wasn't sure. Something felt different with us ever since I got back from sleepaway camp.

I couldn't figure out what it was just yet. We were usually so in sync with each other. But I guess spending some time apart over the summer and going to middle school might have changed things a bit.

It's true that I had no phone or Internet access and so couldn't contact Lindsay all summer, but we're used to that now. We've been out of communication for the past few years when I started going away to camp.

This time I felt different, more than ever before. Even though Lindsay got her first job this summer at Donut Dreams, she was the same old Lindsay that I've always adored. I wasn't sure if she could say the same for me, however.

"So how are you liking middle school so far?" Lindsay asked, changing the subject.

I breathed a sigh of relief, though something in Lindsay's face told me this conversation was far from over.

My best friend always knew when I needed a change of subject, but she never forgot what we'd be talking about.

"Can't say yet," I said slowly. "But it's been okay so far, I guess."

This was our first year at Bellgrove, where Lindsay's mom taught art for years until she died. To be honest, I wasn't all that enthused about attending the school where my mom is the assistant principal.

Okay, I was mortified! I didn't want to be insensitive though and talk about the extent of this with Lindsay, who I'm sure would give anything to see her mom in the halls on the regular.

Now the most visible trace of her mom is a colorful and kind of chaotic mural in the hallway that her students painted in her memory. Basically, the students painted what came to their minds, so the mural was a hodgepodge of storms, rainbows, and wildflowers.

I don't know what the storms and rainbows were about, but Lindsay's mom was a lover of all flowers. Mrs. Cooper was an amazing artist, mostly known for her paintings. She's the reason I fell in love with art.

At Lindsay's house, on one wall of her art studio are paintings of the flowers that she so loved. On the opposite wall are my favorites, these black-and-white sketches of her family. There are some sketches of Lindsay and Sky, and there are also a couple of sketches of Lindsay's dad, too, with a grin as wide as the horizon, as wide as Grandpa Coop's.

I always thought it was so cool that Lindsay had a mom who could draw so beautifully, and how she could take a simple pencil and create such a realistic portrayal of someone she loved. She made it look so simple; with just a few strokes of her hand, she'd make a blank sheet of paper come to life.

A Donut for Your Thoughts

Until I was about six, I was convinced it was magic. Sometimes her drawings looked so real I imagined that they could start talking or walking off pages. Lindsay's amazing mom had a way of making someone's personality and color lift off the page, without using a single drop of paint.

I would watch her make sketches, wishing I could do that one day. It's a wish that has never quite faded like many things do over time.

There was a lull in traffic at the Donut Dreams counter. Grandpa Coop always wanted us to look busy so I straightened the already perfectly straight donuts.

"Who are your favorite teachers so far?" Lindsay asked, wiping invisible crumbs and sprinkles off the spotless counter.

"Ms. Reyes actually makes math fun," I answered. "And our art teacher, Mr. Franklin, was really encouraging when I asked him about doing sketches from my photographs."

"Wait. What sketches? What photographs?" Lindsay asked.

"Oh! I took a lot of photos while I was at summer camp. It was really beautiful there. The trees, the lake, the campfire at night." *Matt's smile!* "Then I started making sketches of the photographs. Now I'm trying to—"

"Oh. I didn't realize you liked making art so much," Lindsay said, cutting me off.

Her voice carried this strange tone that I'd never heard from her before.

"Well, I'm no Amy Cooper," I said. "But your mom definitely inspired me to take up sketching. Then at camp I took a still-life class that taught me so much."

I continued, "So when Mr. Franklin asked us what we'd like to sketch for our first assignment, I showed him my photos and asked if I could do a sketch based on one of my pictures, and he said definitely! He said my photography showed talent."

"Hmm," Lindsay said.

She looked genuinely confused. "I didn't know it took talent to snap a photo. I just click and send."

I wanted to say, *Um, hello. Photography is a legit career. It takes knowledge, talent, and practice to become successful.*

"Well, it's more than snapping a photo, at least for me," I said instead. "It takes creativity and attention to detail. You need to make sure the lighting is good, that your subject is in focus, that it's visually appealing—"

"Visually appealing?" Lindsay repeated.

She rolled her eyes. "You're starting to sound like Mr. Franklin!"

It made me uneasy being compared to our art teacher in such a mean way.

I mean, I wasn't trying to sound like an expert or anything, I was just sharing what little I knew.

Besides with Lindsay being the daughter of an artist, I wasn't sure why she was acting so clueless all of a sudden.

"You know . . . um, you need to make sure that your photo isn't too busy—like, remember that time I took a photo of you in your new dress? You were standing in your room, and there were some books and clothes on the floor, and I pushed them out of the way? I just wanted the focus to be on you—so I simplified the photo," I explained.

"Simplified the photo, wow. I never knew you were so . . . artsy," Lindsay said.

She looked at me with a look I'd never seen before, like she felt betrayed or something, like she hardly knew me at all.

Then she shrugged. "Well, like I said, I just click and send."

I didn't have anything nice to say, so I bit my lip and quietly went on wiping the glass of the donut case. I forced down the lump that had formed in my throat. It actually made me sad that my best friend in the world wasn't really relating to this new and exciting part of my life.

I was glad for the next wave of donut lovers flowing in, since chatting it up with Lindsay at the workplace was not turning out to be as fun as I'd hoped.

Chapter Four
Let Go, Let Flow

That night at the dinner table, my dad was in a super good mood.

As the town doctor, he often comes home from the clinic with deep creases in his forehead that not even an iron could smooth out. Here was a man with the weight of our town's health and well-being on his shoulders.

But tonight he looked years younger. He beamed at Mom as she placed a large bowl of homemade pasta with marinara sauce and a bowl of shredded parm on the table.

I loved the way he looked in that moment, smiling like a boy with no cares in the world.

"Remember my John Doe?" Dad asked as he

spooned out a mountain of pasta into his bowl to satisfy his huge appetite from skipping lunches.

He was talking about one of his recent patients, who'd been hit by a car. Dad's been talking about this poor guy for days.

"We were able to save his leg after all," he told us.

Dad took a confidentiality oath, so he can't tell us who his patients actually are.

But between the vividness of his stories and the smallness of our town, it's easy to put two and two together. Because inevitably, a week from now, "John Doe No Mo" will come hobbling up at the Park or the supermarket with a brand-spanking-new leg cast. A lot of these mystery patients actually come up to me and gush about how much my dad helped them.

I was starting to feel squeamish just thinking about lost limbs and tried to change the subject.

"Mom, this marinara sauce is on point," I said.

"That's great news!" Mom said. She wasn't talking to me, though, but to our dad. "I know you've been worried sick."

"Completely." Dad sighed and then his eyes lit up. "But get this . . . the artery wasn't completely severed, so we were able to connect the healthy tissue to—"

A Donut for Your Thoughts

"DAD!" Gabby and I shrieked.

"What?" Dad asked, like he genuinely had no clue what our problem was.

"We're eating pasta—" I started.

"With red sauce—" Gabby added.

"And you're talking about severed arteries," I said.

"It's über-interesting, Pops, but not dinnertime conversation!" Gabby scolded.

Gabby and I are seven years apart and nothing alike, but we have definitely formed a united front when it comes to not hearing about Dad's surgical adventures at the dinner table. Personally, the stories make me queasy, even when I'm not sending food down the hatch.

Gabby, an aspiring doctor, loves talking shop; she just doesn't think that the table is the correct place for it. Gabby has this thing for polite dinnertime conversation.

As for the extremely gruesome tales of Dad's emergency-room experiences, Mom loves his stories, all day, every day. Why they don't just save the gore for when they are alone is a mystery to me.

"I find your surgeries fascinating," Mom said to him. "And I'm so glad Mr. McKin—I mean, um, John

Doe will be strutting out of the hospital on both legs. That's the most important thing, that he's getting a renewed lease on his life and limb. Bravo, Dr. Peters!"

By the look on Mom's face, she wanted to kiss him, I could tell. Instead she took in another forkful of penne pasta.

But just before her face changed, I grinned at my assistant principal mom smiling like a high school girl crushing on my brainiac dad. I imagined it's how she must have looked when they met at a party all those years ago.

Soon enough, she slipped back into assistant principal mom mode and changed subjects almost as smoothly as Lindsay.

"Gabby, how was your day?" she asked.

"It was okay," Gabby said, jumping right in. "I don't think I stretched enough before dance. I trained hard today too. My legs feel kind of sore."

I don't know how Gabby balances her passion for dance with the demands of college. She was a straight A student all through high school.

On every report card, I usually get a B or two, but she gets mostly As.

Really and truly, my grades are still higher than

most of my friends, but Gabby already set the bar in our household, so I always catch shade from Mom on report card day.

"Ice packs and a warm salt bath for sore muscles," Dad suggested, between bites.

"I've told you a million times you need to warm up before class. You could strain something or pull a muscle—" Mom started.

"Don't I know it," Gabby agreed, cutting her off.

She's a master at shutting Mom down before she can go too far.

It would probably take me another few years to develop that superpower.

"I just get so impatient with stretching. It's like I can't wait to get out there on the dance floor. But I've learned my lesson . . . again. Okay, enough about me! How was your day, Casey?"

"It was decent," I said. "My highlight was getting to work at Donut Dreams after school, which means I made more money to put toward a new camera lens and some art supplies."

"What happened to the lens that came with the camera?" Dad asked.

"It didn't break, did it?" asked Mom.

"Nothing happened to the stock lens," I assured them. "Most photographers have several. Some lenses are better for shooting up close, and others, like the wide-angle, are great for capturing more scenic pictures."

Dad nodded, looking sort of impressed.

Mom narrowed her eyes.

"Ooh, big-shot photographer!" Gabby cheered.

I shushed her and kicked her foot under the table, trying not to smile through chews.

When it comes to art, I guess I'm what you would call a perfectionist, which is not a characteristic of mine in other areas of my life.

For years, I've been pretty private with my artwork because I didn't think it was really good enough to show anyone. But since we've grown up in the same house and everything, Gabby has caught more glimpses of my failed artwork than anyone.

Over the years, she would come visit my room randomly and see one of my clumsy drawings, which I would later feed to the paper shredder in Mom's office downstairs.

I wasn't one for leaving a paper trail of my failures. The only ones I kept were the ones that didn't make me cringe, but even some of those weren't very good.

I guess I could see why Lindsay was surprised by my passion for art.

My camp's art class was life-changing. I mean, don't get me wrong, it wasn't like I turned into Claude Monet overnight or anything like that (he was Lindsay's mom's fave), but that class made me see how good I already was with no formal training.

With a few weeks of practicing every day, my sketches began to take on a whole new life.

Okay, I don't want to brag, but they went through the roof! Since then, I've been focused on getting better and better.

Even though Dad and Gabby were concentrating on their food, I could tell that Mom hadn't had her full say yet.

Until I started getting straight As like Gabby, she would not be satisfied with a single one of my report cards.

"I've never heard you sound this knowledgeable about your core subjects," Mom said.

Core subjects. Gosh.

These days, Lindsay and my mom were starting to have more in common than I ever thought possible, with these jabs at my inner artist. Couldn't they just be happy that I was finding myself?

"I'm doing good in all my classes, Mom," I assured her, keeping my tone light.

"But I'm sure you already know that."

Seriously. Surely Mom was behind the scenes, checking in with my teachers on the regular. Not in an overbearing way like she was here at home, but in brief exchanges by the coffee machine in the staff lounge, casually asking about me between sips.

"Well, I just want to make sure you're doing well in what you're supposed to be studying, that is, your academics, and not just . . . recreational subjects." Mom stressed this with a casual brush of her hand.

"I heard that!" said Dad, who never goes against Mom.

"Low blow, Mom," murmured Gabby.

When Mom shot her a look, she zipped her lips, but not her innocent grin.

Leave it to Gabby to tell it like it is, and somehow make it out intact without a five-point lecture from our mom. Meanwhile, Mom and I always managed to lock horns, especially these days. And I was struggling to fix a problem of mine. It had to do with my emotions, which tend to overheat and cause me to either blow up or shut down.

When someone gets me heated—usually Mom, who lives under my skin—I don't say anything at first, and I let my feelings pile up until one day they all topple out of my mouth in one irreversible mess.

Up until the last year or so, I was much worse off because there was no buildup; I would just turn weepy or go defensive. I was like a time bomb that went off before it even started ticking.

Good thing "ugly-cry-face Casey" hardly shows up, thanks in part to Gabby's coaching. Gabby's helped me get to this point where I can sometimes respond to our mother by just keeping quiet, rather than fighting with her about everything.

Now Gabby's "cope with Mom" techniques are starting to become a little more second nature to me. Like in this case, where Mom ruffled my feathers during polite dinner conversation, the best tool was to focus on my breathing and nothing else.

I took a deep breath and counted to four on the inhale, four on the exhale. It really did kind of help. I let Mom have the last word and just concentrated on breathing and digging into my pasta, which now unfortunately was cold and tasted like cardboard, by the way.

I glanced at Gabby, who was beaming at me like a proud parent as she mouthed, *Woo-sah*.

If I wasn't so annoyed at Mom, I would have had a laugh attack just remembering how Gabby liked to sit on her bed, cross-legged and eyes closed, pinching together her thumbs and index fingers on each hand in a "calm yogi" stance as she exhaled, "Woo-sah!"

I repeated Gabby's mantra in my head, *Let go, let flow*. I was still heated, but I guess you could call it taming my dragon.

Next, Gabby is going to teach me techniques for expressing my hurt or sadness or whatever without getting all tongue-tied and emotional. Like Gabby says, I could be saying something completely valid, but if I'm ugly crying then all the other person will hear is my sadness instead of what I'm actually saying. She has a point there.

I loved watching Gabby, Ms. "It's Not What You Say, But How You Say It" play our parents. She was always showing me that you can say basically anything with the right tone and word choice and actually come out on top!

A Donut for Your Thoughts

I told Gabby she needed to write a book with her expertise. Whether she ends up becoming a bestselling author, a prima ballerina, a doctor, or all three, the world is Gabby's oyster. Whatever she decides to do with her life, our parents will be proud.

I was secretly hoping to make art my career, but maybe it was best to keep that on the hush for just a while longer.

Ugh. First Lindsay and now Mom doesn't understand or appreciate what I want to do with my life.

Chapter Five
Boundaries

The next day at school, I hustled into the cafeteria and plopped down into my usual space at the lunch table next to Lindsay. I was a little late after talking with Mr. Franklin after art class.

Our friend Michelle sat across from us in her wheelchair. I waved at Lindsay's cousin Kelsey, who sat at the next table over with her field hockey and soccer friends.

I glanced over at Michelle's food. She was already scarfing down her ever mysterious vegan lunch.

Lindsay waited for me as usual to unveil hers in our game of lunch telepathy.

"What took you so long?" Lindsay said when I sat down.

A Donut for Your Thoughts

I shrugged.

"Fine. You guess first," she said.

"Fine," I said, looking at her wrapped meal and then deeply into her eyes. "Turkey and dijonnaise mustard on whole wheat?"

Lindsay unwrapped her sandwich to reveal . . . turkey dijonnaise on whole wheat!

"Yes!" I air-guitared. "Your turn."

"Hmm . . . it's a Tuesday, so, let's say . . . your mom's amazing chicken salad on rye?" she guessed.

"Ding ding ding!"

We giggled like dorks as I unwrapped my lunch and we swapped sandwich halves.

I could see Kelsey grinning and rolling her eyes at this pastime we've managed to keep up since kindergarten.

"So did you ever hear back from Matt?" Lindsay asked.

I nodded. "LOL," I said.

"LOL?" Lindsay repeated, confused.

"Yep. 'LOL'—that's all he texted back," I said.

Lindsay shrugged and took a bite of her turkey sandwich. She always liked to save my mom's chicken salad sandwich for last.

"What?" I asked.

"Well, you said you sent him a funny text. So . . . LOL is a perfectly legit response."

"I guess," I said, a little dejected.

Then why did I feel rejected? Lindsay didn't know Matt, so I didn't expect her to get it.

But after getting to be such good friends with this cool boy at camp, I just wished he texted more than three letters at a time. Not that I was expecting a whole paragraph or anything, but I wanted at least some tiny window into his life.

Instead I hadn't been able to inspire a full sentence out of him since we left camp. He wasn't exactly ignoring me; he was just being so super casual. Almost like I meant nothing to him, even though I knew that wasn't true.

Or did I? A familiar lump started rising in my throat, the same lump I've learned to swallow for years.

I turned to Michelle. "Hey, Michelle, are you going to the field hockey game this Saturday?"

Michelle nodded happily. "I need to take some photos for the school website."

"Maybe I'll join you," I said. "I think it would be

fun to sketch some of the players in action."

"Hold up," Lindsay said. "I thought you were on still objects. When did you graduate to sketching people . . . in motion?"

I could tell there was a little shade in her tone, like she didn't think I could do it.

"You don't learn unless you try," I said, leaving it at that.

Lindsay gave me a long look, then opened her mouth a bit like she was going to say something else. But she stopped herself and instead shrugged and took another bite of her sandwich.

I didn't get into the deep conversation I'd had with Matt at our last campfire night before camp ended. Or the countless hours I've started to spend lately in my room obsessing over every feature of my photography subjects, studying anatomy and sketching different body parts over and over, eyes, legs, collarbones.

At first, my subjects looked like aliens with gangly arms and oversize heads. Now my human sketches were finally starting to look amazingly . . . human.

I was just about to bite into Lindsay's turkey sandwich when I heard a familiar voice behind me.

"So what do we have here?"

I didn't have to turn around to know whose voice that was. My face went hot.

"Hi, girls. Hey, honey," my mom said.

"Hi, Assistant Principal Peters," said Michelle.

"Hiya, Mrs. Peters!" Lindsay called out.

"Hi . . . uh," I said, still not sure what to call her.

"I see you girls are still sharing your lunches. I'm sorry to rain on your parade, but your pastime of swapping food is not permitted at Bellgrove Middle School. With so many food allergies going around these days, school administrators decided it's better to be safe than sorry. As you may remember, this was discussed at orientation."

"Oh, I forgot all about that," said Lindsay.

"But we aren't allergic to anything!" I protested, surprising myself with my own loudness.

One . . . two . . . three . . . four . . . inhale. One . . . two . . . three . . . four . . . exhale.

"It's in the school handbook, Casey. There are no exceptions," Mom said with one of her sharp looks that let me know she meant business.

With that, Lindsay took my half of her sandwich from me, gave me back my half, and continued eating.

But I was furious.

"But Mom!" I wailed.

Some boys at a nearby table turned and laughed.

"Rules are rules," Mom said, before walking away.

"It's okay, Case," said Lindsay.

She patted my shoulder and struck up a conversation with Michelle when she saw I wasn't saying anything.

Fuming, I ate in silence for the rest of lunch period.

When lunchtime was over and I stood up, the boys at the next table mimicked, "But Mom! Mom!"

I ignored them, wondering how I was going to draw some boundaries at school between me and my assistant principal mom. Because this wasn't going to work.

Ugh. This sort of thing was everything I'd ever feared. I couldn't wait for this day to be over.

Chapter Six
Boys Are Clueless!

Later that night, after I finished all my homework, I was alone in my room, staring at my cell phone like all the answers to my questions were locked inside.

Mostly, I was thinking about Matt.

What's he doing right now?

Is his home life crazy or what?

Is there something or someone new taking up all his time?

Another girl, maybe?

Doesn't he miss me . . . even a little bit?

I had sent him a sketch of the campfire at camp that afternoon, hoping that it would warm his heart and maybe jog his memory of the long talk we had in front of it.

A Donut for Your Thoughts

Even though I hardly heard from Matt, I was constantly being reminded of him. I mean, I couldn't even walk past a pack of marshmallows in the grocery aisle without some memory awakening. Like the night he toasted marshmallows for me by the bonfire. He didn't even like marshmallows, but he knew I loved them.

"I'll cook, you eat," he said, roasting each one to crispy perfection before handing off the stick to me.

I also remembered the night he inspired this fire drawing of mine. The first thing I noticed about him at orientation was a black notebook he was carrying around. It reminded me of my own trusty sketchbook. In fact, almost every time I saw him, he was holding that black notebook.

After weeks of friendship, I finally had the courage to ask him what was inside it. The bonfire was blazing that night. It was mesmerizing, how the flames licked the night sky.

"Oh, this?" he said. "I'm just writing the story of my life."

I didn't know what I'd been expecting, but not that. I laughed, and his face changed into a defensive mask.

Matt had a bit of a chip on his shoulder, and I kind of liked this about him, because I did too.

"What's so funny about writing down some of the details of what happens in my life?" he asked.

"Sorry, I didn't mean to laugh at your hobby. I think it's actually kinda cool," I said, and I meant it.

"First of all, it's not a hobby, and I'm not doing it to be cool. I'm doing it to stay sane," he said. Then he looked at my sketchbook. "So…what you got going on over there?" he asked.

"I hear you," I said. "Meet my therapist, Ms. Sketchbook."

Matt laughed and flashed a sly grin.

"Can I get a peek? Come on! Let's swap notebooks," he suggested.

That stopped me in my tracks. I'd never shown anyone my notebook before, not even Lindsay.

"Okay, but seriously just for a minute!" I said.

It was going to feel like showing someone my heart and soul, but at the same time I was dying to get a peek into this boy's world.

"Okay, bet," said Matt. "Book swap, go."

Opening Matt's writing notebook felt like falling into a Netflix series. His handwriting was really hard to read, so I had to squint a lot, and I didn't always know who or what he was talking about, but in that endless minute I was shocked to learn that a boy my age could go through so much and have so many feelings.

I was amazed by how many pages he filled with up with life stuff. My life was nowhere near as interesting. I wondered if I would ever be added to his pages, if I would ever be a supporting character.

After a minute we traded books again.

"So what did you learn about me?" he asked.

His face looked almost . . . nervous.

"That I'll need a magnifying glass to decode that chicken scratch of yours!" I blurted.

He laughed, looking relieved.

"You know," he said, watching me in a new light, "I'd secretly guessed that you were really good at something. I was right."

"Oh, you're just saying that," I said.

"Hey, if your drawings weren't amazing, I wouldn't say anything. But they are just that good," he said. "What inspires you?"

"Photographs," I said. "I draw off photographs that I take of everyday things."

"That's cool," he said. "Hey. Have you ever frozen a memory in your mind? When I write, I paint the memories with words. Sometimes I want to explain a scene exactly as I remember it, like how crooked someone's smile looked, or how wild the sunset was the day my uncle died. Description is not my strong point, but I'm getting better at it.

"I bet you could do something similar for your drawings. Then you wouldn't need photographs as inspiration."

"How do you . . . freeze a memory?" I asked.

"Well, what I've had to learn to do is basically pay attention to everything!" Matt said with a laugh. "And every now and again an image will come my way and I just know it's something that I'll want to remember for the rest of my life.

"That's when I take a mental picture. I look at it with my full concentration, tuning out everything else around me. I just focus and snap the picture. Then I keep remembering it over and over again. That's how it begins to freeze."

"Wow" was all I could say.

This sounded complicated, but I wanted to give it a try.

A Donut for Your Thoughts

"Okay, let's make that our homework from camp. Let's choose something from this scene to take a mental picture of to draw or write about. Deal?"

"Deal," I said.

So for the rest of our time by the fire, I tuned out everyone else around us, since some of the remaining campers were still milling about in groups and clusters, roasting marshmallows and the like.

My eyes kept going back and forth between the fire and Matt, the fire and Matt, wondering which mental picture would come out the clearest.

Fast-forward to this afternoon, weeks later, back in Bellgrove, in the grocery store with Mom. I came across a bag of marshmallows and of course thought of him.

I sent Matt a sketch of the campfire when I got home and texted him.

> Remember this? You cook, I'll eat.

It took him hours to respond.

> Coolio.

He's truly the king of one-word responses.

What irked me the most was that I knew Matt could write. When I looked at his notebook, I could tell he noticed details most people didn't.

So how could a boy who knows how to capture a moment so perfectly with his words, not have anything perfect to write back to me?

I couldn't help but feel that there was some kind of miscommunication happening. Just like with everyone else in my life.

I was scrolling through our old texts when Gabby breezed into my room, holding up two dresses. She had just come home from dance practice, looking so carefree and happy. I took a mental picture.

As a dancer, Gabby's bun game was always on point, and her long neck didn't hurt that elegant dancer image. Since our white mom had curly hair and our black dad had straight hair, our hair texture was destined to have an identity crisis. Most days, I couldn't put my hair into a neat bun to save my life, so I resigned myself to making the messy bun work for me.

"Okay, which one?" she asked, holding up the dresses. "For the party this weekend."

One dress was a deep sapphire blue with an empire waist, and the other one was classic black with an asymmetrical hem.

Something I appreciate about my older sister is how much she appreciates my fashion sense! My mood lightened as I envisioned my sister at the party in each dress.

Though Gabby can never go wrong with black, I preferred the way the sapphire blue brought out the deep brown tones in her skin. I decided not to tell her this, because Gabby feels some kind of way about being the darkest girl in every classroom and at every party. I actually admire Gabby's mocha skin, and she just happens to be the most beautiful girl anywhere she goes. Some guys get it, and some don't.

"I'd say go with the blue," I said. "I like them both, but unless you wear a lot of funky accessories with the black, it might seem a little too dressy, like you're trying too hard."

Gabby studied both dresses for a moment, then nodded at me.

"You're right—as usual. Blue it is! Thanks."

She was about to leave when she took another look at my face.

"You okay?" she asked.

I glanced at my phone again and sighed.

Gabby was no stranger to the universe of boys. They've been giving her grief for a long time. This made her super easy to talk to about this stuff.

"Are all boys clueless?" I asked.

Gabby laughed.

"Pretty much," she said. "Why do you ask? Is there one actual boy making your life miserable?"

I nodded. "My friend Matt from camp. When we were together, everything was so great. He's cool and funny and we shared things. But since I've been home, I've gotten exactly three texts from him in response to my reach-outs. And they were exactly one word each. If you consider LOL a word."

"Please tell me you didn't torture him with any cat memes," Gabby said.

I lowered my eyes.

"I couldn't help it, it's a reflex."

"You and your BFF are the only people on this side of the planet who think those are actually funny," Gabby pointed out.

"Hey!" I said. "I got an LOL, okay?"

"Ha!" Gabby laughed, and sat on the bed.

A Donut for Your Thoughts

"Anyway, as I was saying . . . that's the thing about camp: you're far from everything and everyone that's comfortable and familiar. So any real connection you make there is going to be super intense. You two shared stuff in common, right?" she asked.

I nodded and gestured to a picture of Matt, tacked to my bulletin board.

"He was new to camp this year, a scholarship kid. So that was different. But get this, he's biracial too, except his dad left when he was two, so he doesn't really know him," I said.

"There you go! I'm sure that being so alike and also so different made your connection extra intense," Gabby said, examining the picture. "He's cute. And you both have the same skin tone, too."

I nodded.

Matt and I both share that in-between skin color that some biracial kids have, somewhere between beige and brown.

"But since you mention it, I think it was our differences that made us tick. I'd never met anyone like him before, and he'd never met anyone like me . . . that's what he said."

"Yes, but now it's back to reality," Gabby said,

"and he's home with people and things that are really important in his everyday life. Like his friends, his family, heck, maybe even video games—"

"Video games?!"

Was she serious?

I didn't remember Matt mentioning anything about video games being a passion of his.

Gabby laughed.

"Yeah, girl. Haven't you ever met anyone who was a gamer? I made a pact with my heart to never get involved. Those guys can sit in front of a screen and it's over—until the next meal or bathroom break. They are obsessed," she said.

"Well . . . Matt did ask me once if I played Minecraft," I said.

Gabby nodded.

"There you go. Your boy is probably glued to a video screen as we speak," she replied.

I groaned.

"Well, if that's true, and I'm not a hundred percent certain that it is, why doesn't he just text me and say he's busy doing that?" I asked.

"Says the world's best communicator," Gabby said.

She winked and I shut my mouth.

A Donut for Your Thoughts

"I'm just teasing, but not really. Look, the bottom line is . . . he's a boy. And boys are clueless," Gabby continued.

And with that, Gabby hopped away to her room, leaving me to ruminate over what she had just said.

Was Matt really as clueless as the other boys in my grade?

Or was it me?

Chapter Seven
Heart-to-Heart Talk
With Dad

That Saturday my parents made their delicious hot honey shrimp and waffles to jump-start the weekend. I came downstairs to find them cooking up a storm.

Gabby sometimes joked that if Mom and Dad ever decided to ditch their careers to open up a restaurant, they would put the Park out of business. With Donut Dreams in the equation, I wasn't so sure about that.

At the stove, Mom was sautéing shrimp in a skillet, and Dad stood at her side, in front of his old-fashioned waffle griddle.

I stopped in the kitchen archway, and before I knew what I was doing, I was taking a mental picture.

A Donut for Your Thoughts

It was a rear view of Mom and Dad standing hip to hip at the stove, laughing together at one of their many inside jokes. Watching them so in love reminded me of something Matt said to me at camp after listening to me complain about my parents for over half an hour.

He shrugged and said, "Well they sound like angels to me. I haven't heard you say a rotten thing about them yet. You just have no idea how good you have it, that's all."

I now understood what he meant, and it made me see my parents in a different light, a lucky light. I watched them work around each other in our homey kitchen like it was a dance they'd been practicing for a lifetime.

The way Mom could sense that Dad was going to reach around her for a dishcloth and leaned forward at just the right moment. How he opened the fridge to take out the fresh strawberries and left it, knowing she was going to close it with her heel. They each had their job and helped each other out without stepping on each other's toes.

Hashtag cooking goals.

"Morning, Case. I'm on driving duty this

afternoon, so you know what that means," Dad called over his shoulder.

YES! That meant he was taking me to the field hockey game on his day off.

This was great. Mom and I could use a break from each other anyway. After weeks of being together on the way to and from school, only to see each other in school, and at home . . . well, as they say, absence makes the heart grow fonder.

I laughed.

"What it means is, you won't have driving duty later, so Mom will be the one taking Gabby to that party," I said.

Gabby, who was still upstairs getting her beauty rest, is always going to some lake outing or party. That's because she basically gets anything she wants from our parents.

Her secret is no secret at all. Gabby is so amazing at everything she does—dance, academics, her ballet bun—that our parents would feel bad for denying her anything.

Mom turned around and grinned at me.

"True story, Casey. Your dad made sure to negotiate that one first thing this morning!"

A Donut for Your Thoughts

Mom and I laughed. We all knew Dad absolutely dreaded driving his gorgeous daughter to parties where boys were present. His overprotective dad side always kicked in and he always said he had to fight the urge to turn the car around and take Gabby home.

After family brunch, Gabby and I washed the dishes and cleaned up. Then it was time for me and Dad to go to the game.

That afternoon was a beautiful Saturday for field hockey. It was perfect fall weather—the air cool and still, sun high, not a cloud in the sky.

As we settled into Dad's SUV and buckled our belts, he glanced down at my sketchbook and seemed like he was about to say something, then decided against it.

I side-eyed him. I knew why he wasn't going to go there. If he was even slightly interested in the fact that I was bringing a sketch pad to a school sporting event, well, there was no way he was going against Mom who said I should be spending more time on "academics."

After all these years, Gabby and I have never been able to come between our parents on any front, and Gabby's a pro. They are so united on every possible thing, it's like they possess this weird parental telepathy. They're such different people in the world, but when it comes to me and Gabby, it's like our two parents merge into one. I personally found it super annoying, but then Matt came along and showed me another perspective.

Back at camp, I thought Matt and I had some sort of telepathy going. By the last week, we were finishing each other's sentences and saying the same expressions. Then camp ended, and poof, he fell off the face of the earth, like the imaginary friend you suddenly outgrow.

After his last one-word text, I didn't really know what else to say without coming off as too "in my feelings"—even though I was! So I remained silent.

And then there was Lindsay, who I've had a telepathic friendship with since kindergarten, until just lately. I didn't know what was happening with us, but we weren't so in sync these days either. It was like we'd lost our radio signal and there was all this static between us, interfering with our connection.

I was losing my grip on two people I cared about, and I wanted to know my parents' secret recipe for relationship success once and for all. Despite their busy lives with competing responsibilities, how did they manage to stay so . . . in sync all the time?

I was just about to ask my dad about this when he interrupted my thoughts.

"So what are we filling our ears with this morning, Miss DJ?" Dad asked, fiddling with the Bluetooth on his phone.

I was so lost in thought I almost didn't answer. Usually, I decided what we listened to when Dad drove me, but music was the last thing on my mind today.

"I dunno. Whatever you pick, I'm game," I mumbled absentmindedly.

"Well, that's a first," Dad said, before choosing his favorite Otis Redding playlist.

He started the car and backed out of the driveway.

"Dad . . . do you and Mom agree on everything?" I asked, once we were well on our way.

"Heck no, we don't always agree," he answered with a laugh.

"For real?" I asked, disbelieving.

"Well, you and best buddy Lindsay are practically married. Do you two always see eye to eye?"

"Definitely not," I grumbled.

Especially not lately.

"Well, same goes with your mom and I. We're not always of the same mind on things and have to talk it out behind the scenes. Thankfully, our home is spacious enough, or else you'd hear us."

He paused before adding, "Especially when it comes to you and Gabby. As the parents, we must find common ground, or else you two queens of schemes will walk all over us!"

Dad and I laughed hard at this for a good minute because it was so true.

Gabby alone would debate our Mom and Dad all day and all night if necessary to get her point across.

Dad continued, "But what I'm saying is, we don't always agree on issues that bubble up concerning politics, religion, and the two of you, but when it comes to our children, we have to land on a position. Through the process of doing this since you were babies, essentially, your mom and I merged into our own organism."

Ha. After blowing my mind with his honesty, leave it to Dad to put his scientific spin on everything.

"Can you two read each other's minds?" I asked.

Dad laughed loud and looked away from the road

for a half second to throw me a glance.

"Sorry to disappoint, but we have no such abilities. Your mother is one of the greatest mysteries of my life, next to science. I don't think I'll ever understand her completely.

"Yet, over time, we've learned to accept each other for exactly who we are. Years of disagreeing to find our middle has made it easy in our later years to predict what the other's response will be to any question or situation you two come at us with."

"Now this is one real-talk Saturday," I said.

I still didn't get it all, but I couldn't wait to tell my sister the good news, that Mom and Dad didn't have telepathy after all.

※　※　※　※　※

The field hockey girls were doing warm-up drills when we arrived. I scanned the first row of bleachers for Michelle. When I spotted her, she was already waving me over from her wheelchair at the far end.

I sat in the front row with Michelle, and Dad sat a row behind me to cheer on our team. He's really into sports and gets really loud at games, so I never let him sit next to me.

"I've already gotten some great shots. Check these out," Michelle said excitedly.

She handed me her camera to take a look.

"Michelle, these are amazing," I said.

There were some wide shots of the girls stretching, and more close-ups of them talking with their coaches. Michelle had zoomed in on their faces so you could see how intently they were listening to every word their coach said.

I felt especially inspired by photos of the girls laughing and fooling around. I wondered how well I would be able to capture all that personality with the mental pictures I was planning to take, plus my pencils.

My favorite was a photo of Kelsey that was really incredible. She was holding her hockey stick laughing, lots of blue sky above her and a look of pure joy on her face.

"You can see how much she loves to play," I said. "This could be the cover of a sports magazine!"

Michelle grinned.

"Thanks. That's my dream, actually! I want to one day see a photo of mine on the cover of a magazine," she said.

A Donut for Your Thoughts

"Keep taking photos like this and you'll be well on your way," I assured her.

With a smile, Michelle looked through her camera lens and started snapping away again.

The game started. We became quiet for a while, each of us deep in thought.

I turned to a blank page in my sketchbook and glanced at the players. Sophia caught my eye. She was small, swift, and dark-haired, and played with a fierce intensity. That made her a great subject to draw, but also a challenging one. She moved like a minnow on the field, making it harder for me to pin down a mental picture. It took me a while to latch onto something, but once I did, it was exhilarating to capture her energy on the page.

After a few minutes, Michelle leaned over to peer at my sketch.

"Now that's amazing," she said, then laughed. "Sophia looks so serious, doesn't she? You almost want to give her a hug and tell her to lighten up."

I beamed, silently overjoyed that Michelle knew exactly who I was sketching, and that I'd done Sophia justice.

"That's why I thought she'd be great to sketch.

I loved the expression on her face." I turned to Michelle. "Since I got back from camp, you're the first person to be interested in my artwork, so thank you for saying that. Sometimes I struggle with whether I'm even any good. But I've been working really hard to hone my craft. I guess it just feels good to have my work . . . seen."

I surprised myself, saying this much to Michelle. She was more Kelsey and Lindsay's friend than mine. I guess I was feeling more comfortable talking about this with someone who shared an eye and appreciation for life's beautiful moments.

"Yeah, I could tell you weren't feeling it at lunch the other day when Lindsay was just not getting it," Michelle said.

"Oh, you noticed, huh?" I asked, laughing.

Michelle smiled.

"I have an eye, remember?" she said, holding up her camera. "Casey, you're not great at keeping your feelings hidden. Even if you don't say what you feel, you're saying it anyway."

"Good to know," I said.

"Look at it this way," Michelle said, lowering her camera and turning to look at me. "Sometimes, people don't get things they're not interested in. My cousin Joanne wants to be a physics teacher. Physics! I break out into hives just thinking about math. So you know, to each her own."

She raised her camera again and took a few more photos. Then she added, "And you know what else? I think Lindsay might be a little jealous."

"Jealous? Why?"

"Her mom was a great artist. I'm sure Lindsay would love to have a little of talent herself. But you have talent."

"Hmm." I was silent for a moment, considering this. Lindsay and I have never had problems with jealousy in all our years of friendship. She didn't ever seem to be jealous about me going to sleepaway camp every summer, and Lindsay wanted nothing more than to leave our small town, where anybody's business is everybody's business.

Michelle continued, "Don't get me wrong— she's not crazy jealous. It's not like she hates you or anything like that! I'm just saying I think she feels a little uncomfortable when you get excited about your artwork. It probably reminds her of her mom or something."

I sighed, because she had a point.

"You know, you might be right. I never thought about it that way," I said.

"You should talk to her about it," Michelle said. "It's never good to keep things bottled up. She's your best friend, after all."

I nodded. "Maybe I will."

I know Lindsay's my best friend, but still, why do I feel so uncomfortable?

Chapter Eight
Cute With a Capital C

The following Monday at lunchtime, the girls' field hockey team huddled around Michelle at our lunch table. From the outside, it could have looked like they were strategizing their next play. But really, they were gazing at Michelle's photographs from their game on Saturday.

"Shelly, you always make me look *sooo* good!" Kelsey squealed. "I want a copy of this picture."

It was the photo I loved too, with Kelsey gripping the hockey stick and laughing with the blue sky.

"If you think these are good, you should see Casey's sketches. They're even more amazing," Michelle said.

Before I knew it, the girls were grabbing at my sketchbook.

Now with the spotlight suddenly on me, my face went hot with embarassment, which then turned to pride. Since the art exhibit at the close of summer camp, I haven't had a chance to show my artwork to anybody. I've been pretty secretive about it.

"Wait, wait! Hold up!" I said, laughing.

I was kind of happy that people were actually interested in my work for a change. I opened my sketchbook and flipped some pages, looking for the field hockey sketches.

A sketch that I had torn out of the book fluttered to the floor. It was meant to be private, but it was already too late.

"Now *you* hold up—who is this?" Kelsey said, picking up my sketch of Matt.

I hadn't planned to show it to anyone. Actually, I had torn it out to put it someplace private but got sidetracked.

I hadn't drawn it from a photograph like the others before it, but from a mental picture of my campfire memory of Matt. I had to close my eyes for a long time until every feature of his face froze into place and made sense. I had tried to remember him on paper, but it didn't come out exactly as I saw it in my mind. No matter how good or bad the drawing was, it could never capture Matt in living color.

But even my drawing of his dark hair, sparkling eyes, killer smile, and deep dimples had a table of girls captivated for a few moments.

I guess that meant I'd done something right.

Matt had that effect on all the girls at camp too, but he was only interested in spending his kayaking and campfire hours with me. Maybe it was because I was biracial like him, or the only girl who wasn't fawning over him.

It felt kind of awesome seeing people so mesmerized by my sketches but I also felt super exposed, as if everyone, just by staring at the picture, could overhear our campfire conversations and taste the marshmallows Matt roasted just for me. It was like everyone was reading from a ripped-out page of my private journal.

"CUTE, with a capital C!" squealed Sophia. "Is that your boyfriend?"

I sighed inwardly.

I wish! Or do I?

"I'm not even allowed to have a boyfriend, Sophia. We're just friends," I said.

"What's his name?" Michelle asked.

"Matt."

"Ooh, Maaaaatt," said Sophia, drawing out the sound of his name and making the rest of the girls giggle.

Kelsey put the sketch down on the cafeteria table, and Lindsay leaned in to take a look.

"So this is Matt-who-never-texts-back, huh? He's cute, I guess," she said.

My face was burning up.

"He texts back. Just not . . . a lot."

Kelsey sighed.

"He's dreamy, Case," she said. "Why aren't there any guys who look like this around here?"

"We need to get them imported," Michelle joked.

The rest of the girls exchanged high-fives and laughed.

"Hi, girls. What's so funny over here?" asked an all-too-familiar voice.

I froze.

How long has she been spying?

"Hi, Assistant Principal Peters," some of the girls said in unison.

"Hi, Mrs. Peters!" Lindsay perked up.

A Donut for Your Thoughts

Funny, Lindsay hardly ever looked this excited to see me anymore.

"Casey, I was just sitting in my office, thinking that it's been a while since we invited Lindsay over for my famous lasagna," Mom said, looking at her with a smile.

Don't assistant principals have other things to think about? I thought.

Mom waved a manicured hand.

"What do you say, Linds, would you like to come over for dinner tonight?"

"Ooh, that's so nice," said Sophia.

"Jealous!" Michelle half joked.

"I have to ask, of course, but I'd love to!" Lindsay said enthusiastically.

In a sudden movement of excitement, she knocked over a container of juice . . . all over my Matt drawing. The bottom half of my sketch got soaked.

All of the girls gasped in horror.

"Matt!" Kelsey cried out dramatically, as if he were really drowning.

"Wait? What?" Lindsay said, clearly embarrassed.

Thinking quickly, Michelle grabbed her camera and snapped a photo of the sketch.

"I'll send this to you and you can print it out," she told me. "Just lighten the part that's darker because it got wet. Good as new."

I didn't say anything, just took a napkin and gently blotted the wet part of the sketch. I realized then that how much the sketch meant to me.

Kelsey looked at Lindsay. "Gosh, Lindsay. Can't you at least say you're sorry?"

Lindsay shot me a look, but I noticed she couldn't hold my gaze for more than two seconds.

"She knows I'm sorry . . . don't you, Case? Like Michelle said, you can print out a new copy. Or you can just whip up a new sketch."

I fumed.

Whip up? This is not a kitchen and I'm no Betty Crocker!

"What do we have here?" Mom asked.

With all the commotion, I had forgotten that she was even there. She leaned down to look at the half-wet sketch and then looked at me with a raised eyebrow.

"Clearly this is your handiwork. Who's the boy, Case?" she asked.

"Nobody, Assistant Principal Peters! It's just a

stupid drawing I whipped up . . . right, Lindsay?" I shouted.

Tears stung my eyes, threatening to fall.

I quickly scooped up my sketch and sketchbook and rushed out of the cafeteria, leaving my lunch, and probably a lot of confused faces, behind.

Chapter Nine
That's the Tea

After school, I sat outside the closed door of Assistant Principal Peters's office, as usual, waiting for a ride home.

If a stranger were to walk into our school at that moment, I would probably look like some troublemaker waiting to get detention. But the truth is, I've never gotten in trouble at school a day in my life, and there are no strangers in Bellgrove.

My science teacher, Mr. Sanders, smiled as he strolled to the school exit.

"Put on your game face, Casey," he said, laughing at my frown. "She'll be out any minute."

I forced a smile until he disappeared out the door, not taking a mental picture, but making a mental note to find another place to wait for Mom.

How could I possibly cheer up after the most embarrassing day of my middle school existence? It was bad enough having the field hockey team gawking at my top secret drawing of Matt, but to have my assistant principal mom popping up whenever she felt like it? I sent up a silent prayer to please make it stop.

A few minutes later, the office door opened and a few teachers streamed out. They all greeted me before heading for the exit.

Assistant Principal Peters drifted out, looking pleased until her eyes fell on me. Maybe my stormy expression made her smile shrink just a tad.

"Ready, honey?" she asked.

"Ready," I said, standing.

Mom grabbed her jacket and car keys.

"Okay, let's jet," she said.

On the slow drive home, the air inside Mom's car was so thick you could cut it with a butter knife. Mom tried to make small talk, about the beautiful fall weather, and the upcoming games, but like Matt, I could only manage one-word responses.

There was definitely an elephant in the car with

us, something that was obviously important to talk about, but difficult to bring up. If I were Mom, I'd be trying to figure out the best way to bring up something uncomfortable, without getting the usual defensive response from me. She knew she was treading on thin ice as it was.

Talking things out without erupting, or without my emotions spilling all over the place, was such a chore. It made us both uncomfortable, and we knew that too. I just wanted to run from it all and be left alone to sort out my tangled mess of feelings with the help of my therapeutic sketchbook.

My phone buzzed. I had a new text. I glanced down at it, my heart pounding.

It was Michelle.

U ok?

I sighed and texted back.

Yes. Thanks for asking. TTYL

I was happy Michelle had texted me, but where was Lindsay? Did she not even care that she had ruined my sketch? As if this day couldn't get any worse, my BFF was not even texting me.

Halfway home, we had to stop at a railroad crossing. This freight train was moving at the pace of a sloth. Leave it to the most awkward car ride of the year to become the most epic.

I looked out my window, even though there was nothing interesting to see. Even though I couldn't see her, I could feel Mom staring at me.

She sighed.

"So are you going to tell me what that outburst at lunch was all about?" she asked.

Here it comes. Mom wasn't one for beating around the bush like Dad.

My head got blank and my lips refused to move.

But Mom didn't let up.

"Casey? Are you upset with me for some reason?"

Fair question, I had to admit. When I really thought about it, Mom technically didn't do anything wrong as a parent. Okay, she didn't appreciate my love of art, and that stung. And I definitely wasn't cool with her rolling up on me at school whenever she felt like it.

However, when I thought of her reason for today's lunch-table visit, she actually meant well.

I usually loved having Lindsay over for dinner, almost as much as I loved my mom's lasagna. But after what happened at lunch, I actually would have appreciated a little space from Lindsay. Which felt kind of icky, because I've been totally crazy about Lindsay for as long as I can remember.

So, tangled up inside, I became tongue-tied.

The sloth train continued to crawl past, and I started fidgeting with my almost-curls.

"What's going on in that beautiful head of yours?" Mom asked.

She hesitated when I didn't answer, and then continued, "Sometimes it's like pulling teeth trying to get you to tell me how you feel. Just remember that no feeling is too big or too small because all feelings are important and deserve a voice. Especially when someone is showing their willingness to really hear you."

Mom sure knew how to get me thinking.

These days I can't tell big feelings and small feelings apart. I don't even know how much space any of my feelings should take up.

Is it big or small that the people closest to me don't give a hoot about my passion in life?

A Donut for Your Thoughts

That my BFF might possibly be jealous of me?

Is it big or small that Matt ditched our friendship to play Minecraft or maybe for another cool girl?

That my mom is my assistant principal and I feel like I can't sneeze without her showing up out of nowhere with a box of tissues?

I guess the point my mom was making was that the size of my feelings doesn't matter. The important thing is that I have them and can share them with a welcome ear if I want to. It isn't easy to open myself up to my mom, because I feel she always expects perfection from me.

As for Lindsay, who used to be my walking diary? Since her mom died and especially since I came home from camp this year, much less.

My dad? Maybe if I got to spend more alone time with him.

Truth be told, my sister Gabby is the only one who knows me fully and totally accepts me. I don't want to run to my big sis for every little thing, but knowing that I can if I want to means plenty.

It would've been nice to have that level of comfort with my mom, but she sometimes makes it hard, with her own strong opinions on things having to do with me. While some kids say their moms are bulldogs, mine's a bulldozer.

Sometimes I feel like she's trying to demolish my own opinion of myself, to build it back the way she wants.

Clearly this sloth train isn't going to let me off the hook either, so . . .

Suddenly, I turned my head to lock eyes with my mom. I never noticed that we were the same height sitting down.

I looked at her and saw her, us, and, well, everything so differently. It was like this invisible veil between us fell away. We looked at each other as if we were seeing each other for the first time. I had to take a mental picture because never had my mom looked so beautiful.

Is my bulldozer mom . . . emotional?

Her eyes were a little wet, and I could see in them her love for me. I saw warmth, worry, regret, confusion, fear.

Whoa. My mom was actually, officially, certifiably in her feelings! Maybe in our private universes, most of us are.

I took a breath and went for it.

A Donut for Your Thoughts

"Ever since I came home from camp this summer, I feel like nobody gets me anymore," I said.

Mom zipped her lips and studied me.

"I also feel like I've changed . . . like, a lot. I think I grew up at camp this summer more than usual. I was excited to come home as this changed girl. But at home, nobody seemed interested in all the cool things I learned there. Everybody was on their back-to-school grind, and then pretty soon, there was this feeling that I never went anywhere at all this summer. Except I felt so much different, so much clearer about who I am because of what I'm passionate about.

"I want to talk about art to every person I meet. I like to take photographs of interesting things and capture precious moments in my mind and develop my photographic memory. I love to draw people and study their faces and bodies and how they move.

"I feel like people who've known me forever understand me the least, and people I hardly know see me clearly. It's confusing to be afraid to tell the people that I love most that I want to be an artist and nothing else. I think I'm already an artist, and I want more than anything for you, Dad, and Lindsay to see that. I want you to be proud of me for being me, not some mini version of you.

"Artists do all kinds of interesting things with their lives. I want to do art with my life! I don't know what that means exactly, because I'm still figuring that out, but I believe that whatever I decide to do, I can do! I used to doubt myself so much, and for the first time I actually believe in myself! And it's all because of art!"

I took a deep breath and looked at my mom. She was still looking at me, expecting me to continue, so I did.

"I used to say that I would follow Lindsay out of this town to the ends of the earth just so we could keep swapping lunches for the rest of our lives. I came back from camp not feeling that way anymore. Don't get me wrong, she's still my best friend. But I don't really know if I want to go away and live in a big city like her.

"After art school I feel fine about staying close to home, but I would like to make an interesting life for myself as an artist wherever I end up! I want to scream out this window, 'I am an artist!'—even if no one hears. I want this to be a hashtag fact in our family from now on."

"Hashtag fact?" Mom asked.

By then, the train had passed and the light turned green. We were finally moving forward.

"Oh, just some social media lingo, learned it at camp." I waved it off.

After saying my piece, I already felt better and was even breathing easier.

"Hashtag, oh, okay, gotcha." Mom nodded, filing that one away in her brain.

She was a middle school assistant principal, after all, and needed to stay in the know.

"Wow. I'm listening to you, Casey. Go on," she said encouragingly.

"That's really about it." I shrugged.

I didn't know what else I wanted to say. I was amazed that I'd said that much without blubbering all over the place. I was just happy to know that lightning didn't strike or that waterworks didn't come just because I shared my feelings.

"How's that for pulling teeth, Mom?" I asked.

Mom couldn't help but laugh. "I mean, phew, Casey." She smiled before she said, "You sure put me in my place with that soliloquy. I knew you had it in you, not to tell me about myself, but to tell me about yourself. Thank you so much for telling me how you feel. You really do have a lot going on in that big brain of yours."

"I know!" I laughed. "And so much more."

"I bet," Mom said.

I could actually hear with those two words that she'd heard me, everything I'd said.

She took a deep breath and let it out.

"Okay, my daughter the aspiring artist. I'm sorry I didn't take you seriously in the beginning. I guess a large part of me saw art as a passing phase in someone's life until reality hits. One day you'll have bills to pay and a family to support. I think it's difficult for artists to pull that off, especially in a small-town setting like ours. But then, I always have to remember that the world is changing.

"I also have to remember my friend Amy Cooper, the beautiful, important artist," Mom said. Her voice filled with emotion then.

We shared a few moments of silence, misty-eyed as we remembered Lindsay's mom, whom everyone had cherished and loved.

"I miss her," I said.

My lip quivered as I pictured her angular face and

soft features in my mind. She was beautiful, inside and out. I could see her so clearly in my mind's eye that I could almost smell the lavender and see the shade of blue she always painted with and wore. That and her wind-chime voice always filled me with this safe, calm feeling.

I never told Lindsay that it still made me endlessly sad that her mom was no longer here. I couldn't imagine how Lindsay must feel to wake up every day without her own mother.

I looked at my mom's profile as she drove us home, and something about the way the afternoon light was hitting her round face and her curls reminded me that she was not just a bulldozer, but a beautiful bulldozer, more beautiful than words could say.

As much as she got on my nerves, I couldn't imagine life without my assistant principal mom. I could do without the assistant principal part, but that would be the same as her saying that she could do without the artist part in me.

I knew what I had to say to her next.

"Casey, I love you," my mom was saying. "Your life is your show. As your coproducer, I want you to be who you are meant to be, but you better work your butt off to be successful at it. Don't let me or anyone get in the way of your dreams. As long as you continue to maintain your grades, I will support you one hundred percent in your artistic pursuits. If your grades begin to slip, you will be hearing from me. Fair?"

I breathed a large sigh of relief.

"Fair. Thanks for hearing me out . . . this time. There's something else."

Mom sat up a little straighter in her seat and nodded, keeping her eyes on the road.

"I want to apologize for being such a sourpuss about you being the assistant principal of my school. I came into middle school with a bad attitude that created my responses to certain things. I should be more grateful and proud to say you're my mom. I can't speak for kids in the older grades, but my friends at school admire and respect you. A friend from camp this summer has helped me see how ungrateful I've been. Sorry, Mom," I finished.

"This means a lot to hear. I accept your apology," Mom said.

Her eyes scanned the road as she navigated the more congested part of town, close to the Park. She wiped away a tear with the side of her hand.

"I now understand why you combusted on me at the lunch table," she said.

"I mean, in the middle of having friend drama—" I started.

"Here comes your assistant principal, inviting your friend home for lasagna," she finished.

"Without even asking me first!" I added. "How rude. What if Lindsay and I were in a fight or something? What if I had a ton of homework?"

"Valid points." She nodded. "I'll make sure to check in with you first before inviting your friends over. Deal?"

"Deal," I said. "Well, at least you didn't invite Lindsay over for fish sticks. You had all the jocks so hungry for your lasagna, no one was paying attention to just how lame I felt!"

We laughed long and hard.

"I guess we do need to set up some boundaries at school," Mom said, after catching her breath.

She then fell quiet as she thought for a moment.

"How's this?" she suggested. "No chatting on school grounds unless it's something important and school-related. From now on, when I see you anywhere at school, I'll just wave unless you stop to talk to me first. How does that sound?"

I considered this with a smile.

"Do you have to wave? Can't we just work on our mother–daughter telepathy?" I asked, half joking.

Telepathy with me would be impossible!

"Casey! You're my daughter! I'm not going to ignore you if I see you! That would draw even more attention."

I sighed. "Yeah, that's even weirder. Okay to wave."

"Deal," Mom said, turning onto our tree-lined street.

She parked the car in our driveway and turned to me.

"Are there any other feelings you want to share, about anything at all?"

"My mug isn't empty, but I think I've spilled enough tea for one day," I said.

I hugged her.

"Thanks, Mom," I said.

"Thank you for being so vulnerable with me just now," Mom said. "You taught me something today."

"It wasn't easy to speak up at first, but once I started, it felt really good," I said.

A Donut for Your Thoughts

Next up, Lindsay.

Just then my phone signaled that I'd gotten a text message. This time my heart didn't speed up, hoping, wondering if it was you-know-who as I pulled out my phone to check.

"It's Lindsay," I said. "Turns out she can't come over for dinner tonight."

Phew! Because I feel like I've just run a marathon!

Chapter Ten
The Big Surprise

That week, instead of going to lunch, I stayed in art class a few days to work on a new drawing that had me quite obsessed. I was starting to like spending more time in the most vibrant and inspiring classroom in school.

Our art teacher, Mr. Franklin, had an open-door policy during lunch hour for student artists. Anyone working on independent art projects could go to his room during lunch period, and Mr. Franklin pretty much left you alone to do your thing.

He didn't helicopter the room like in his regular art class. Instead he just sat with his feet up at his desk, chomping away at his lunch and jamming out on his cushiony headphones.

A Donut for Your Thoughts

That Wednesday, I texted Lindsay to let her know I wasn't coming to lunch . . . again.

> Finishing something up in Franklin's room today. Lemme guess . . . pastrami & swiss on pumpernickel?

> Yup.

Sheesh.

If Matt was the king of one-word responses, Lindsay was joining him on the throne.

Things weren't the same with us these days, and it was my fault. We both knew we were long overdue for a heart-to-heart, but I wanted the moment to be just right.

Mr. Franklin was my favorite teacher for a number of reasons, one of which was that he had turned Mrs. Cooper's old room, now his room, into a constantly changing art exhibit.

Actually, if you really think about it, you can spot examples of art almost everywhere in school, thanks to the art department that Lindsay's mom directed for years: from the self-portraits that line the long wall on the way to the library to a ceramic octopus sculpture at the main office sign-in desk. And of course there's the funky mural in the main hallway that's dedicated to Amy Cooper.

My favorite is the painter's palette that she always used, which Mr. Franklin suspended from the ceiling of his classroom with fishing wire. At least once a week, usually before class starts, I stand still in front of the hovering palette, spotted with paint colors.

I gaze up at it for a few seconds, I don't know why exactly, just to send up a prayer. My way of remembering her, I guess.

Something about the palette being in midair makes me imagine her on the other side wearing angel's wings, floating above us as we make art in what used to be her classroom.

I also feel close to Lindsay's mom every time I talk to Mr. Franklin.

He can sketch and paint, too, but he's more into collage work and bookmaking. He's mostly known for these awesome, one-of-a-kind handmade books with collages on the cover, which he sells online.

What I didn't know until I started talking to

Mr. Franklin was that Amy Cooper had been his mentor for many years. Actually, he says she's the only reason he is an artist at all.

We definitely have that in common, because I feel the same way about her.

"Hey, Casey, I want to talk to you about something," said Mr. Franklin.

The door was wide open to welcome any other lunchtime artists, but for now, the room was empty.

Once I reached the front of the room, Mr. Franklin picked up Twin Flames, my first sketch from memory of the campfire, which I'd recently turned in.

"Casey, this is wonderful work," Mr. Franklin said, smiling at me.

He pointed to the campfire flames and continued, "I'm halfway convinced that I can warm my hands over this drawing, it's that good."

I laughed, a little embarrassed. But I was touched by the compliment, especially since I really admired Mr. Franklin as an artist.

"I'm so glad you like it! Most people might look at it as a stupid fire, but I actually spent a lot of time on it," I admitted.

"Well, I am not 'most people' and can see your

potential a mile away in just one of these flames," Mr. Franklin replied.

He waved a hand over my sketch and said, "Your eye for detail is incredible. It actually inspired an idea I have for the school website."

"What idea?" I asked.

"Well, how would you like to submit sketches for the site? We could call it 'A View from Bellgrove,' or whatever better thing you can suggest. You can sketch friends in everyday scenes like lunch in the cafeteria, competing in sports, or chilling in the hallway.

"Of course, you'd need permission from anyone you decided to sketch—especially with the realism of your sketches.

"But I think it would be fun and interesting to show a student's view of the school, and maybe we could expand it to include photographs as well— from you and from other students. But I'd like you to head up this visual component of the website and be in charge of it. It might mean staying after school a few days a week to do it justice."

I was floored by Mr. Franklin's offer, which was a perfect solution to a number of problems.

Seeing that I only got called into the Park as a

flyer every once in a while, I had been wanting to do something after school that was more productive than sitting around waiting for some clueless boy to get back to me. Besides, I was waiting around aimlessly after school for Mom for up to an hour these days anyhow.

Now I would be able to fill that time doing something worthwhile.

"Mr. Franklin, I would love that!" I said.

I thought about it some more, and then suddenly, I had a great idea.

"My friend Michelle is a really great photographer. She also would have a lot to contribute," I told him.

"Yes! I'm familiar with her work," Mr. Franklin said, smiling.

I beamed back.

"Let's loop her in, and you can curate this together with her, if you want," he continued. "Let me talk to our website designer, and we can start moving on this right away. I think this will be a very nice endeavor for you, Casey."

He paused before adding, "And it's never too early to start thinking about college. I'm sure people will be impressed when they see you had your artwork featured on a website at such an early age."

DONUT DREAMS

I might not have been jumping up and down, but I was so thrilled, like, surprise-birthday-party thrilled.

This would be a great way to show everyone that art was around us, all the time. That artwork was important and should be appreciated.

I couldn't wait to tell everyone the great news.

Chapter Eleven
In Our Feelings

That evening Dad and Gabby teamed up on the cooking, which always led to a delightful meal.

Sometimes Dad came home a little later from work than usual, so he would ask someone here at home to start the process of preparing dinner, like chopping up vegetables.

That was fine by me. I was happy to contribute in a small way because I can't cook to save my life. My dad teases me that I can't even boil water for a cup of tea. I find it hard to concentrate on measuring ingredients, or timing a recipe.

But Gabby was no sous chef. Whenever she started dinner, she would end up putting her own spin on Dad's original idea.

Dad's Southern roots make him a hopeless BBQ romantic, and Gabby loves Asian cuisine, so ... steamed shrimp wontons and Hunan barbecue chicken were on tonight's menu.

I mean, with a whole house smelling this good, no one had to call me downstairs for dinner. I was already in the kitchen hovering over wontons by the time dinner was served.

"Another patient came into the emergency room last night after being hit by a car." Dad sighed.

He shook his head as he carefully spooned some coconut-baked candied yams onto his plate.

The creases in his forehead were way pronounced. From being on call at the emergency room for so many years, Dad's seen it all, but he never stops caring about each and every patient.

"Another one?" Gabby said. "Why are so many people being hit by cars these days?"

"There are more geniuses on the road who think it's a good idea to drive while texting," Dad answered.

Mom added, "Girls, take this as a reminder to never cross a street right after the walk signal comes on. Always wait a few seconds and look both ways before crossing."

A Donut for Your Thoughts

"It happens all the time. A split second could cost you a leg or your life," Dad said. "Last night's Jane Doe came to us in such a state of shock she didn't realize how badly the car had damaged her until she looked down at her leg and saw that her bone was exposed—"

"Dad!" Gabby shouted, looking down at her drumstick.

Usually, I was right there along with Gabby shutting Dad down, but this time I kept quiet.

Something was different this time. I was different. Instead, I was creating a mental picture of my dad in this moment that happened so often at our dinner table, and I noticed something new.

A crumpled expression that I'd never seen before rippled over my dad's face. In that millisecond, Dad looked similar to how I felt after being totally misunderstood by the people closest to me. My mind started racing.

What if my dad, the town doctor, also felt like a total reject . . . at his own dinner table (which he built, by the way)?

What if coming home from work, for him, was like coming home from summer camp for me?

How did it feel to be the town hero coming home to your kids, who didn't want to hear the gory details of your lifesaving days in the ER?

I guess I hadn't been fair to my father, either.

"Excuse me?" Dad said coolly. "What happens during my day should also have a seat at this table."

Gabby and I looked at each other with wide eyes and closed mouths.

Whoa. I'm now convinced that we are all in our feelings!

I spoke up.

"Dad's right. Five minutes of Dad's day is way more important and exciting than both of our school weeks combined," I said, reasoning with Gabby. "I should be able to forget my silly sensitive stomach for a few minutes of dirty details at dinner."

With that, I popped a wonton into my mouth and started chewing.

Gabby nodded, agreeing.

"So what did you do with the exposed fracture?" she asked Dad.

I tried to compose myself as Dad went on to unfold the whole gory scene in great detail.

"So how was your day, Casey?" Gabby asked,

smoothly changing the subject the instant Dad seemed to have gotten it out of his system.

"Mine was great!"

I told them about my exciting conversation with Mr. Franklin.

"That sounds wonderful, Casey," Dad said, glancing at Mom and tossing her a wink.

"Congratulations!" Mom added. "Soon you'll be making a name for yourself at Bellgrove. Get ready, because people are going to start commissioning you with candy bars to feature them in your drawings!"

We all laughed.

"They better come with more than just candy bars," I joked. "My services aren't cheap."

We laughed some more.

"Look who's feeling herself . . . Ms. Artsy," Gabby teased me, with a slight shove.

"Casey, would you like to show us some of your artwork sometime?" Mom asked.

"Woo-hoo! Art showing!" said Gabby.

"I'd love to."

I beamed. I couldn't wait to show them my newest sketches, all created from memory.

"I don't mean to put a damper on things, but

your story could explain why Lindsay was looking so glum in the lunchroom today," Mom said. "Have you two gotten a chance to talk since last Monday's BFF drama?"

That grabbed Gabby's attention, and her eyes went wide.

"Who has drama? Lindsay and Casey?" she asked Mom. She shot me a curious look and waited for an answer.

I sighed, pushing the food around on my plate before I said, "We haven't talked yet." I felt a bit ashamed to admit it.

Mom did have a point, though. No wonder I was getting only one-word answers from Lindsay. I'd gotten so involved with my latest drawing that I totally fell off the map with little explanation. Lindsay must have been feeling confused.

I would definitely be salty if she did the same thing, especially with how different our friendship was feeling since middle school started. Heck, we couldn't even swap sandwiches anymore thanks to the school rules!

"Sounds like you might want to remedy that soon," Dad suggested.

"Well, can I hang out with Lindsay after school tomorrow, please?" I asked.

My parents shot each other that telepathic glance Gabby and I knew all too well.

"Sounds like a terrific plan," Mom said.

Chapter Twelve
The Two Artists

That night after dinner, I texted Lindsay.

> **BFF hang after school tmrw?**

My heart was beating quickly . . . like every time I ever texted Matt.

What if she was already too mad and totally rejected me?

A minute later, Lindsay texted back.

> **Sure.**

I smiled. Finally, a one-word response that was music to my ears.

A Donut for Your Thoughts

The next day I asked Lindsay to meet up with me after school in the art room before walking over to my mom's office together.

Mr. Franklin agreed to make himself disappear, so we had the room to ourselves for at least half an hour.

Even though this had been Mrs. Cooper's room for so long, Mr. Franklin had done a good job of making the classroom his own universe. Just the vintage Woodstock posters alone are enough to transport you into a different decade each time you walk in here.

Everywhere else you look is student art galore. Mr. Franklin is a total enthusiast about displaying student art in the freshest ways possible, even hanging pieces from the ceiling to catch the eye.

Mrs. Cooper's palette would be there forever, but it was cool to see the art constantly changing.

We entered the room and stopped just short of Lindsay's mom's floating paint palette and stared up at it.

"You know what will be the hardest part about leaving Bellgrove?" Lindsay asked.

It's no secret that she feels stifled by small-town life and has always had her sights set on bigger, faster places where no one would know her life story. Where she could just melt into any crowd.

"You'll feel like you're leaving her behind?" I guessed.

"That's why you're my BFF," said Lindsay.

She squeezed my hand.

It was good to know that even after weeks of weirdness, there were some things Lindsay didn't have to explain to me.

Now I had some explaining to do. I could feel the usual traffic jam of words in my throat begin to form, so I took some deep breaths and felt the congestion clear.

"Listen, I know I haven't been the best BFF lately," I said.

Lindsay's eyes widened.

"OMG. I haven't been the best BFF either!" she exclaimed.

"Okay, who wants to go first?" I chuckled.

Clearly we both had some explaining to do.

Lindsay raised her hand.

"This summer, I was actually secretly jealous for the first time when you went to sleepaway camp and I had to stay in Bellgrove," she said. "Then you came back like this whole new person, with lip gloss and a boyfriend and talking differently and acting more like my own mom than . . . well . . . me! I was also surprised by how good your drawing was. I didn't even know you liked to draw!"

"That's my fault," I said. "Your mom's been my inspiration for as long as I can remember. When we were little, I used to watch her sketch you and Sky. I think she even made a sketch of me once. It was mesmerizing to watch her blank sketchbook fill with captured moments in just a few pencil strokes. I used to leave your house wishing my mom had a superpower like yours did.

"The older I got, the more I wanted to be just like her. I was seven when I started drawing, but I thought my sketches were too horrible to show. I didn't show my sketchbook to anyone until summer camp this year."

"Lemme guess . . . Matt?" Lindsay said.

"Like I said, I haven't been the greatest BFF." I smiled sadly.

I then explained to Lindsay how Matt and I ended up swapping notebooks for a whole minute just because we were curious about each other.

"For being such a cutie, he had sort of ugly handwriting." I laughed.

"I'm sure he wasn't ready for how amazing your drawings are," Lindsay said softly.

"Thanks for saying that. He kinda wasn't!" I agreed.

"Well, he sounds as dreamy as he looks," Lindsay said. "I'm happy for you."

She smiled.

"It was fun while it lasted. He completely fell off the map. Oh well." I shrugged before I added, "I was really sad at first, but now I'm just a little sad. Hopefully soon, I won't be sad about it at all. It's good to be busy with other things, anyhow."

"I've noticed," said Lindsay, looking around Mr. Franklin's room. "You sure have been spending a lot of time in here. What have you been up to?"

I told her about Mr. Franklin's idea to curate "A View from Bellgrove" using my drawings and photographs from other students.

"Casey, that's fantastic!"

Lindsay's eyes lit up, and I could tell that she was genuinely happy for me.

"This gives me an actual reason to visit the school

website. You might need to give it a cooler title than that, though," she said.

"You might be right about that," I said thoughtfully, wondering what other title would be more ear-catching.

I told Lindsay that I'd been busy working on the first sketch for the series.

"I'd like to publish my first piece with your permission," I said.

"My permission?" Lindsay was clearly surprised.

She followed me to the annex room, where Mr. Franklin stored student works.

I found my large folder and pulled out a finished portrait, the one I've been obsessing over for the past week. I put it in Lindsay's hands.

She gasped, and her hand flew to her mouth.

"I know I've been MIA lately, but I wanted this drawing to be just perfect, to come out exactly as I saw it in my mind," I said. "It's not perfect, but I hope it's good enough. Do you like it?"

I was a little nervous while I waited for her answer.

Lindsay's eyes welled up as she stared at my sketch of her mom, who was smiling directly at us from the other side of life, wearing angel's wings.

"Casey, it's . . ." Lindsay was choked up. "My favorite drawing ever. It looks realer than any photograph I've ever seen of her. I love it. My family would love to have Mom honored in this way. I'm officially obsessed with your talent!"

"I've been practicing drawing from memory, and this is how I see her . . . behind my eyes," I explained.

"Is this what I think it is?" Lindsay said.

She grinned as she ran her finger over the halo I'd sketched above her mom's head.

"A donut halo, Case?"

We laughed our butts off.

"Sorry, I was hungry and couldn't resist," I giggled. "Now the title should make sense."

"'A Donut for Your Thoughts,'" Lindsay read the title at the bottom of the sketch.

We laughed a heap more.

"Perfect," she said.

"I try," I said, grinning from ear to ear.

"Now I feel stupid for being so jealous," Lindsay said. "It's just that I wished my mom's artiness had rubbed off on me, too. She taught me to appreciate art, but I'm pretty sure I'm not an artist. I'll never be as good as my mom."

"I don't think anyone's expecting you to be," I said, trying to comfort her.

"Wrong about that!" Lindsay said. "Since I started drawing stick figures, people have asked me if I'm going to be an artist like her. Whenever I say my last name, people assume I'm going to be a great artist. Then . . . they quickly see how wrong they are. I feel like I'm letting everyone down when I don't churn out some amazing drawing . . . including my mom."

"Wow, Lindsay, I had no idea."

Now it was my turn to be surprised. I guess that goes to show that even though we've been BFFs since day one, literally, there were always things to learn about each other.

Maybe this was what my dad meant when he said that he would never understand my mom completely, even after all their years of marriage.

Mr. Franklin strolled into the art room.

"How are you two doing?" he asked, with a wink.

"Good," Lindsay and I said at the same time.

We looked at each other and started cracking up. Because we were.

"I'm glad I have you here, Lindsay, because I want to ask you something," Mr. Franklin said.

He joined us in the annex room, pulled some work out of one of the large student folders, and came over.

When she saw what he was holding, Lindsay covered her eyes and her face turned bright red.

"Your continuous line drawing this week was one of the best in your class," Mr. Franklin said, holding up a drawing she'd made of her art partner. "Look at how smooth and effortless your line is. Excellent eye-hand coordination."

Continuous line drawings are not my favorite; I have serious problems drawing someone's face in one continuous line without being able to pick up my pencil. Mine come out all shaky.

But Lindsay had done a great job. I could recognize our friend Michelle's face in her drawing, clear as day.

"Thanks, Mr. Franklin." Lindsay beamed with pride.

"I wanted to ask you if I can hang this up. I already have an idea for what kind of frame I want to use to make it pop," said Mr. Franklin. "Do I have your permission to do so?"

"Well, I'll have to think about it," Lindsay said, twirling a lock of her hair and looking up. "Okay! Yes!"

We all laughed at her terrible acting skills.

I nudged her with my elbow. "So, as you were saying?"

Grinning, Lindsay turned and hugged me.

"Okay, I guess it's still possible that I can be an artist."

Chapter Thirteen
Two of a Kind

Later, Mom dropped us off at the Park to continue our BFF date. Everything was arranged for me to get a ride home from the Coopers after dinner.

At the podium, Grandpa Coop greeted us as he did everyone, like we were special.

"Now here's my favorite pair in town," said Grandpa Coop. He always chuckled, for some reason, at the sight of us.

"I know I'm doing something right when my employees show up to work on their day off."

Uh-oh.

Did Grandpa Coop mean work as in place of business, or work as in grab an apron and get cracking?!

A Donut for Your Thoughts

Maybe he thought we were coming in to save the day instead of to hang out like regular customers. What is he actually saying?

I glanced at Lindsay to see what she thought.

She looked back at me with confused eyes that said, *I don't know.*

Her eyes angled toward the Donut Dreams counter behind her, which she'd have to turn her head to see.

From where I was standing, I only had to look straight past her head to see what was going on there.

Lindsay's older cousin Lily was behind the Donut Dreams counter, and that was a sight to see.

Lily was my favorite of Lindsay's high school cousins. She had such a genuine smile and a beautiful nature that made her really good with kids. When she spoke to them, her voice was like a bottle of honey, warmed in sunshine.

If the Park View Table hadn't snatched her up at birth, she would be the town babysitter or something.

Lily also happens to be the clumsiest waitress as well as the most anxious driver I've ever seen. After many broken dishes, she retired from being a server.

Thankfully, everyone in town knows Lily's car

and can look out for her on the big bad roads of Bellgrove.

With the Donut Dreams customers, Lily was keeping the conversation moving, all smiles, but as a worker it was clear that she was super overwhelmed. She almost dropped a fresh tray of donuts, but the queen of close calls played it off with her million-dollar smile.

I gave Lindsay a *sorry* look.

She turned to Grandpa Coop and said, "We are here to rescue Donut Dreams if need be."

It might not be Mom and Dad's, but our BFF telepathy wasn't so bad.

"Thank you, girls, but it's not my call," Grandpa said, glancing at Lily and looking a little relieved. "You know where to find the Donut Dreams powers that be. Why don't you go back there and see what they have to say about the fate of Donut Dreams this afternoon."

Lindsay and I headed to the back to the kitchen, where all the magic happened.

Nans and Lindsay's dad were having a friendly disagreement about something. They looked relieved when they saw us.

A Donut for Your Thoughts

"We're here!" said Lindsay.

"Do you need help with anything?" I asked.

"I need someone to tell Nans here that her taste buds are aging faster than she is," said Mr. Cooper. "I don't know what you're talking about, Mom. This lavender lemon cake donut is my best creation yet!"

Lindsay's dad gestured to his newest donut flavor like he was some game show host unveiling the grand prize. The donut sure looked dreamy, with yellow sprinkles and true blue icing, his wife's favorite color.

Lindsay and I glanced at each other and smiled. I was pretty sure we were both thinking the same thing, that this would be the perfect donut for her mom's halo.

"Not so fast," said Nans.

She was a tough critic when it came to the dream status of new donut flavors.

"The lemon is too loud. I can't taste the lavender. That's false advertising!"

"Well, we have two more judges," Mr. Cooper said, offering us a donut each.

He was looking mighty confident.

"Tell us what you think, girls," he said.

Now here was a donut for your thoughts. I must

say, when you bite into one of Mr. Cooper's freshly made cake or yeast donuts of any flavor, it's hard to be a real critic. The consistency of the lemony cake was perfectly soft and dissolved in my mouth like a dream.

In a minute flat, Lindsay and I were licking our fingers.

"Dad, this is amazing," Lindsay said. "But Nans is right. I don't know if I'm tasting the lavender."

"Neither am I, but I've never tasted lavender before!" I said.

"Same here!" said Lindsay. "Maybe we need one more donut each just to make sure!"

"Hah! Nice try," Mr. Cooper said. "But I think I got the answer I needed. Back to the drawing board I go. Have fun with your BFF on your day off, Linds."

Funny thing: donut making sounded very similar to art making, after all. Maybe Lindsay had more art in her genes than she realized.

When we returned to the floor, Lily had the Donut Dreams counter under control. Streams of happy kids and their parents were flowing out of the Park with bags and boxes of pure sweetness.

Lindsay grabbed our favorite booth by the window,

with a lush view of the park. Minutes later, her older cousin Jenna automatically brought us cream sodas, our favorites.

"Hey, I never got to say how sorry I was for ruining your sketch of Matt," Lindsay said. "I was way too embarrassed to think about how it must have made you feel. And the way everyone was looking at me like I was the worst person on the planet . . . I wanted to disappear!"

"I know the feeling," I groaned. "Especially when my mom showed up."

"Yeah, that must have been pretty mortifying," Lindsay agreed. She gave me a sympathetic look before taking a sip of her soda. "She was all up in your business."

"Who's the boy, Case?" I imitated in my best Assistant Principal Peters voice.

We laughed so hard at my impression that tears started to form a bit in my eyes.

"So what did you do with the portrait?" Lindsay asked. "I hope that it isn't too ruined. Do you still have it in your sketchbook? Can I see?"

I quickly finished the last of my soda before I opened my sketchbook. I flipped through it until I came across the sketch. It wasn't too bad once the OJ dried.

"It was just going to sit around and become yellow on its own anyway," I said.

"You mean, you weren't going to show it to him?!" Lindsay's eyes got huge.

"No way!" I almost shouted. "Why would I do that?"

"Because it's amazing!" Lindsay insisted. "If that doesn't get you more than a one-word response from him, I don't know what will."

Lindsay got me thinking.

Matt was really turning out to be one of those out-of-sight, out-of-mind friends. I was just starting to put our friendship behind me, and I wasn't so sure that I wanted to put myself out there again, and risk feeling rejected . . . all over again.

Matt also lived far away. Our camp is five hours away from where I live and Matt lives five hours away too…but in a different direction. If he didn't land a scholarship, then most likely he wouldn't be at camp next summer and I would never see him again.

Was it even worth it to reach out one more time?

What if he didn't even like the drawing?

"Let me see something," Lindsay said.

Before I knew it she was picking up my phone and carefully positioning it over Matt's sketch to take a picture.

"The damage doesn't show up that much."

She handed me the phone.

The sketch did look pretty legit.

Funny how I'd started out making sketches from photographs. Now I was making photographs of my sketches, and I had Matt to thank for it all.

I supposed sending him the picture of him that I'd drawn was the least I could do.

I thought of that night at the campfire when we promised to create mental pictures from memories. Little did he know that it was not only the campfire burning its way into my mind. His face had snuck its way into the fabric of my thoughts. If it weren't for his encouragement, I'd still be in my comfort zone, sketching from photographs.

Now my memory was becoming sharp, like my dad's old-fashioned razor. If it weren't for Matt, I would never have had the bravery to start sketching from memory, at least not now. In a huge way, Matt played a big part in the artist I am today.

Maybe some thanks were in order.

"Atta girl," Lindsay said, as I went ahead and sent him the picture.

But it felt different this time.

The difference was, I sent it to him without hoping for a response. It was like a wordless thank-you for believing in me when I didn't even believe in myself.

"So what else are you working on?" Lindsay said, eyeing my sketchbook.

Now I was actually excited to show her my newest project, "Two of a Kind."

It was a sketch I was working on of my parents, a back view of them standing hip to hip at the sink. Dad is washing dishes with his eyes on Mom, grinning like a boy, and Mom is drying dishes and watching him, too, all in her feelings.

"Ooh, Case, this is so romantic," Lindsay said. "This is going to make them fall in love with each other all over again!"

As if my mom and dad needed any help in that department.

Lindsay and I looked through more of my sketches and ordered some delicious food to eat.

It felt nice to get back into the groove of our

friendship. I could see what Mom had meant about talking things out. It definitely felt good to clear the air, even though it had been hard.

I could see now that even Lindsay and I were two of a kind.

Chapter Fourteen
Close to Perfect

Later that night, alone in bed, I was putting the finishing touches on "Two of a Kind." I was planning on unveiling it to my family the next morning at our Saturday brunch. I had dragonflies in my stomach just thinking about coming out of my artsy closet to my family once and for all, but I was ready.

My phone buzzed. I guessed it was Lindsay, but no, it was Matt's name flashing across my screen.

He definitely had more than one word this time.

> Hey C. Ur sketch was sooo good I didn't know what 2 say @ 1st. I will never 4get it or u! Thank u!

A Donut for Your Thoughts

By the way my heart was flopping around in my chest, you would have thought Matt had just walked in my bedroom door.

What was up with me?

I thought I was close to forgetting this clueless boy, but also the most mature boy I've ever known. Now all our memories were rushing back, our nicknames and jokes and life talks over blackening marshmallows. If I'm being totally honest, his more-than-one-word response was way more than I'd expected, but why was I sitting there wishing he'd said . . . more?

I guess it was good to know that he'd remember me at least, that he remembered our private joke about our skin deserving its own Crayola color, biracial beige.

Still, I wanted more of a window into his world.

Was he writing as much as I was drawing?

And was school kicking his butt this year or what?

And did he ever think of me before he fell asleep?

If only I could get another peek into his notebook, squinting at his chicken scratch, just to get a clue. Too bad he was so far away.

I stared into my phone for a while, thinking of how to respond. I got up to go visit Gabby's room for boy advice, but I quickly sat back down instead. It wasn't like this was a crisis. I had this.

I belly-flopped back onto my bed and picked up my phone.

> Um . . . never forget me? Are you going on a secret mission to Mars or something?

> LOL I dunno. Just didn't want 2 assume.

> Assume what? That I'm your friend and want to know what's up with you?

> Sorry, Case. Been crazy busy w/ school + Mom's giving me lots 2 write about. Think of u daily, tho.

> Been thinking of you too and busy with new drawings. Just finished one for my parents.

A Donut for Your Thoughts

They'll love it. Still can't get over how much better u got after camp.

Thanks! Tomorrow morning will be their first time seeing a drawing of mine!

I love ur parents + I don't even know them. Can I come + meet them?

Are you for real? They don't know you exist!

LOL! That hurts, ice queen. I told my mom bout u. She loved ur cat meme btw!

. . .

U there?

Sorry, wasn't expecting that. Are you serious??

Yeah we talk bout u all the time. Is that weird?

Um . . . yeah! You talk about me but not TO me??

My bad 4 not telling u sooner. Mom takes my phone 4 no reason! I nvr have time on here. I just got it back 2day after she had it all week!

. . .

Hello?

Crazy, I thought you were forgetting about me.

I couldn't do that if I tried, girl.

Well I tried.

LOL. Fo sho. How'd that work out?

I was feeling all warm and sleepy by the time I put down my phone. For minutes on end, I stared at the ceiling with a silly grin, all those familiar summer feelings coursing through my body like my own blood.

Matt and I had had such a great conversation. It felt just like the summer had—no pressure and no issues. After weeks of worrying over the state of our friendship, I now felt the opposite, that Matt and I were friends for life.

Life suddenly got totally cool and super weird.

Had Matt just invited himself over for a visit? To meet my family?!

And I couldn't believe his mom saw my cat meme!

I was feeling mighty guilty. While Matt and his mom were chatting it up about me, he's been the elephant in my house.

What was my problem, anyway?

Aside from the fact that he was a boy, and a cute boy at that, Matt was hands down the closest friend I'd ever made at sleepaway camp.

Even worse, when my mom spotted his portrait

and asked me about him in front of the field hockey team, I actually called him a nobody.

A nobody!

Maybe I was the weird one. Ugh.

I picked up my phone and texted Lindsay.

> Brilliant BFF for making me send that photo!

> I just got waaaay more than a one-word response and I am not mad at it! 😏 Stay tuned for more Casey tea tomorrow! Love ya!

> LOL! Groan. Ur such a tease. Love YOU!

I couldn't wait to tell Gabby in the morning that her video-game theory was way off.

Back at camp, Matt didn't talk about his mom a whole lot, but I got the impression that they were really close, even though she was super strict and no-nonsense.

One story he told me stood out in particular. One morning he said something disrespectful to his mom on the drive to school, and she pulled over and made him walk the rest of the way.

He was ten!

I couldn't imagine my mom doing something so hardcore, but with my snotty attitude these days, I'm sure she's thought about it at least once.

As for his dad, well, he didn't make sense to me at all, because he left when Matt was two. Matt didn't sound sad about it, though; he was very matter-of-fact about it all.

I picked up the sketch of my parents and studied it, cocking my head to the side like Lindsay's mom used to do when she came close to finishing a painting.

I resisted the urge to pick up my pencil once again and mess with it some more. I was learning that in art there were always things that I could change, or wished I could change. But there comes a point when it's time to let it go.

And while sharing my portrait of her mom with Lindsay was nerve-racking, even though I might not have shown it, the true test was my parents. I felt kind of jittery inside just thinking about presenting this to them tomorrow at brunch. The more I looked at the picture to spot something wrong with it to fix, the more I realized that I didn't want to change a single thing.

In a world where there was no such thing as perfect, this was close enough.

Chapter Fifteen

Matt Meets the Family
(Sort Of!)

Whatever goodness they were cooking up that special Saturday lifted me out of a dream and out of bed and pushed me into the bathroom to brush my teeth.

I trudged into the hallway, and I could hear my family downstairs chatting and laughing—Gabby's laugh drowning out everyone else's, of course. Just listening to them filled me up with that warm, lucky feeling I had only started feeling lately.

It was inevitable that Mom would end up working some nerve of mine, but I wanted to hold on to this feeling for as long as I could.

I tossed some water on my face and looked at myself in the mirror. For once I didn't start fussing with my combination hair. I didn't care that it hadn't yet decided if it was going to lie down straight or levitate, or that today it looked sort of blah.

Today's mirror showed me so much more than myself. It was my mom's round eyes staring back at me, hovering over my dad's nose, the way our nostrils flared when we breathed. When I lifted my chin, I almost had Gabby's swan neck. Almost.

Before going downstairs, I scooped up "Two of a Kind" and gave it a final once-over.

And you know what? The dragonflies in my belly weren't even there anymore.

Of course I still hoped everyone would swoon over my newest work, but that mattered less now, for some reason. But it felt more important that I loved the outcome almost as much as I'd loved making it!

I was also itching to figure out what my next project would be.

"Casey!" Gabby called from downstairs. "Food's ready!"

"Coming!" I called, and galloped downstairs.

Three pairs of eyes smiled my way when I entered the room. Mom, Dad, and Gabby were patiently sitting in front of untouched plates of shrimp and grits.

A Donut for Your Thoughts

"Morning, fam," I said, plopping into my chair.

"What you got there, Case?" Gabby asked, nodding with her chin at my sketch.

Leave it to her to move this thing right along.

This is it.

"Mom, thank you for asking to see my artwork. It meant a lot to me. So I've been working on something all week to show you . . . during my recreational hours, of course, ahem," I said, giving Mom a totally unnecessary, petty sideswipe that made her laugh with surprise.

And that, my friends, is what you call the Gabby effect.

"Shots fired!" Gabby said, looking like a proud mama, giggling at the low-key shade of it all.

"Well let's see this A-plus artwork," Mom responded haughtily, but with a big grin that got us laughing all over again.

When I turned over the page to show off my newest creation, I admit my heart must've stopped for at least an instant.

Mom's hand drifted to her mouth.

"Oh my," she said.

Her eyes were welling up when she looked at my

dad, who was getting a little misty-eyed too.

I considered it a slam dunk, getting both my parents in their feelings at the same time.

"This is us," was all my dad could manage.

"My two and only," I answered, beaming.

"Casey, I must say, this is incredible work," Mom said, snapping back into assistant principal mode.

It made me wonder if I had imagined the whole teary-eyed thing.

"I thought you were holed up in that room of yours doing some cartoon drawings, what do you call those . . . man . . . ?"

"Manga, Mom!" said Gabby.

"Yes, that," Mom said, waving away the matter. "But this is really realistic stuff, Case, and it's amazing. Extraordinary. So meticulous! This must have taken forever—"

"Just every spare moment I could squeeze out of this past week," I said.

"Well done. It's a real level up for you, Case," Gabby said, nodding her head sincerely.

That meant a lot coming from the only person who has seen my drawings grow from stick figures.

"I see a bright future ahead for you and your art,"

Dad said. "It's actually inspired an idea that I hope you'll say yes to, as long as it doesn't take too much away from your schoolwork, of course. You would also earn some dollars to keep up with your art supply bill."

Well, that got my attention.

"I'm listening," I said.

"I've wanted to do something to make people more aware of the perils of texting while driving, sort of like a PSA. And after seeing the realism of your drawings, this came to me. With their permission, of course, can I commission you to do portraits of survivors of text-related accidents? I would like to feature their portraits in and around my office to humanize the PSA. What do you say?" Dad asked.

My turn to be in all my feelings. I was speechless.

Without saying anything, I got up to hug my dad.

Then Gabby got up for a three-way hug.

Mom must have been feeling a little left out, so she wrapped her arms around all of us.

"End scene!" Gabby called out, making us explode into giggles as we took our seats.

She picked up "Two of a Kind" and placed it on the counter to protect it from shrimp grease.

"Let's dig in!" she said.

"So, Case, do you have any more work that you'd like to share with us?" Mom asked, heaping shrimp and grits onto her fork. "I'm hooked!"

If I could raise an eyebrow like a movie star, I would've, because I definitely wasn't expecting that from my mom!

"I do have another thing," I replied, beaming, and whipped out my phone.

Oops.

Lindsay had sent me a text two hours ago dying to know what went down last night.

I flipped to my photos and showed them the sketch of Matt. They approved of the picture, but would they approve of the boy?

"This is Matt Machado, a boy I met at camp," I said.

"A boy?" my dad said slowly, as if it was just dawning on him that I hadn't been attending an all-girls sleepaway camp for the past five summers.

He clearly hadn't gotten the memo, but Mom wasn't surprised. I knew she remembered this picture from the cafeteria.

"Handsome young man," Mom said, nodding.

"Looks interesting, too. When will we have the pleasure of meeting him?"

"OMG, he said the same thing in a text message last night, but I thought he was mainly joking," I said. "Truth is, he lives pretty far away. And he is interesting, since he's a writer and all."

"Ooh, a writer and an artist! What an interesting pair you must've been at that boring ol' sleepaway camp!" said Gabby, totally rubbing it in.

"Text . . . last night?" Dad repeated in a sort of daze.

"Earth to Dad!" said Gabby, waving her hand in front of his face. "No worries. He's just her camp friend. Right, Casey?"

"He's not just my camp friend," I said.

The room went quiet.

"He's my camp BFF!" I finished.

"Hmm. I wonder what the Bellgrove BFF would have to say about that," said Gabby.

"Nice try, Lindsay already knows," I said.

Gabby was always finding ways to make me and Lindsay argue, mostly because she thought our best friend drama was hilariously cute, even cuter than cat memes.

"If you say he's your BFF, then we're going to have to meet him eventually," Mom said and looked at Dad. "Right, hon?"

"Well, I don't see why that's even necessary," Dad huffed. "And doesn't he live far away?"

Gabby and I looked at each other. Had Dad just disagreed with Mom openly?

"Um, there's something called video chat," said sweet and sarcastic Gabby. "We can beam him in right now if we wanted."

And as if by magic, my phone lit up in my hand and sounded.

"Speak of the devil," I said.

It was Matt texting.

Hey C, wanna say hi 2 my mom?

Yeah, but only if you say hi to mine too.

Ha! Mom swap! I'm game if u r. Let's go!

A Donut for Your Thoughts

"Is everyone ready to meet Matt and his mom?" I asked.

I took an extra-long look at Dad, and he nodded.

"Beam him in," he sighed, quickly wiping his grease-lined mouth with a napkin.

I answered Matt's request to video-chat, and just like that—Matt and his mom were at our table.

"Hey, everyone, hey, Case, meet my twin!" he said.

He put the camera on his mom and we all laughed, waved, and said hello. His mom really was just a darker and more beautiful version of him, with short, dyed locks.

And before we could say anything else, our moms hit it off, just like that. Somehow, they started talking about everything under the sun all at the same time! They talked so much that my hand was starting to ache from holding up the phone for so long.

The last time I saw Mom speak so candidly with someone outside of our family was, well, with Lindsay's mom. Clearly, they needed to exchange digits and talk on their own time.

Before we all hung up the phone, Matt's mom said to me, "Matt told me he met an artist at camp, and boy, he was right. He showed me your drawing of him, and I must admit, I got a little teary-eyed."

"Well, yes, we're now just learning Casey's art does have that effect," Mom said. "We've been unaware."

"Speak for yourself and your husband," Gabby laughed. "I've always known my little sister had crazy talent!"

Matt's mom laughed and rumpled his hair. "Talking about talent, my twin here shared the story he wrote about you two, Case, and it brought tears to my eyes."

"Mom!" Matt groaned.

And I thought my cafeteria scene on Monday was the height of embarrassment!

"Story about *moi*?" I said.

Then I remembered the night at the bonfire when we talked about mental images, and the deal we made to re-create a campfire moment using our photographic memories, no cameras.

Matt's mom said that when I sent Matt my campfire drawing, he got to work on re-creating our scene for the book of his life.

Matt promised to read it to me later on.

"So does that mean I'm officially a character in your book?" I asked.

A Donut for Your Thoughts

I couldn't hide my blushing any more than Dad could hide his dismay.

"That's entirely up to you, Casey, because in my son, you've got a fan," Matt's mom said.

I glanced at Gabby, who just about melted.

After we said our goodbyes, I couldn't wait to put down the phone and dig into the rest of the delicious meal my parents had made. Even though I was packing on hundreds of calories, I felt a thousand pounds lighter.

And I couldn't wait to call Lindsay. It seemed like everything had finally fallen into place.

As I ate and laughed with my family, I couldn't help but smile at everything that had happened these past few weeks. Who knew so many changes could be like, so totally rewarding!

Now I was an official artist, I had learned to appreciate my awesome family, and I had not one, but TWO BFFs!

Chapter One
The New Normal

I woke up this morning feeling totally at peace, even though it was a Monday.

Crazy, right?

But after a few weeks of middle school, I finally felt like I had the hang of things: I knew exactly how long I had to get to each class, where I could hide and take a phone break, and the best locker to grab when I had to change for PE.

One thing I didn't like, though, was that our

seats weren't fixed in all of our classes. In elementary school, my BFF Casey and I would pick our seats right next to each other on the first day of school, and those would be our seats for the year. We could relax.

Now, I'm scrambling to try to get a seat next to Casey at least half the time. And if we don't time it right, we're way far apart. I wish I had the hang of that.

Still, I've kind of been loving the routine of middle school. It's funny, because all of my life I've dreamed about getting out of Bellgrove, my tiny hometown where everyone knows everyone else's business and routines.

But lately, I've been kind of liking it. I've felt happy knowing exactly where I had to be, what I had to do, and who would be with me every day. For the first time, it actually felt good knowing everyone in town and having all of them know me. It felt like things were under control.

Speaking of control, my grandmother's kind (but bossy) voice floated up the stairs and curled under my door. "Lindsay? Sweetheart? Are you up yet? Rise and shine!"

Nans comes over every weekday morning to get me and my brother, Skylar, to school. Ever since our mom died a few years ago, our whole extended family has pitched in to help fill the giant Mom-sized hole in our lives.

My mom's mom, my grandmother Mimi, is our only relative on her side of the family. Mimi lives in Chicago, which is two hours away by car, but she visits a lot and we go see her there often. It's really hard on her that my mom is gone, so we comfort each other in both directions.

My dad's family is from Bellgrove and they all settled here. Our family owns a restaurant called the Park View Table that's like the hub of our town. It's centrally located and overlooks our beautiful town park, and inside it is a small donut shop called Donut Dreams.

Almost everyone in my family has a job at the restaurant: there's my dad, Mike (he runs Donut Dreams); me (donut counter); my grandpa (manager); Nans (chef); my dad's sister, my aunt Melissa (finances); her girls Kelsey (donut counter with me), Molly (a "runner" or bus girl), and Jenna (waitress); my dad's brother, my uncle Charlie (ordering and inventory);

and Charlie's son Rich (waiter) and daughter Lily (hostess).

My aunt Sabrina is a nurse and my uncle Chris is a carpenter who also teaches shop at our town high school, but even they help out at the Park from time to time. We all pitch in together and take care of each other, though lately it's mostly been all of them taking care of me and my family.

All of this has been great for me and Sky and my dad, and I know that. It's just that I really wish my mom were still here. I wish I could have her back, even for a minute, even just to talk about some boring thing in school, or what was going on in her garden.

My mom was an artist, but she was crazy about flowers. She had a beautiful garden out behind our house (it's gotten a little wild, I hate to admit) and she loved planning it and tending it and cutting and arranging its flowers.

My mom often said she could have been a florist almost as happily as an artist and art teacher. "It's the same skill set—shapes and colors!" she used to say.

At the very end of my mom's illness, she told me to remember that after she died, whenever I saw a flower, it would be her saying, "Hi."

And whenever I saw a blue flower (her favorite color was cornflower blue, or "true blue," as she called it), it would be her sending me a huge hug. It's made me notice flowers a lot more, which I guess was her point.

"Flowers bring joy," she would always say. "Seek out joy!"

But now that fall was settling in, there weren't too many flowers around, and certainly not any blue ones. All I'd been seeing were those tubs with ginormous balls of Halloween-colored mums in them, orange and yellow and rusty red.

Yuck.

I missed my mom.

"Lindsay!" Nans called again.

"Coming, Nans!" I whipped off my comforter and scrambled to get ready.

❋ ❋ ❋ ❋ ❋

Downstairs, Skylar was already at the table, eating his bottomless bowl of Coco Snacks, or whatever the flavor of the week was. The kid is always starving, and Nans lets him have junky cereal for breakfast because it makes it easier to get him out of bed that way.

"Some call it bribery," Nans would sigh when asked. "I call it time management."

My morning job was to get our lunches ready while Nans fixed breakfast. Since our family owns and runs the Park, we're all pretty comfortable in the kitchen.

Nans was making me a quick omelet, just the way I like it with cheddar and chives, while I made ham and cheese sandwiches on whole grain pita pockets with mustard and baby spinach for me and Sky.

I wrapped them in our new reusable Bee's Wrap waxed cloth (my dad's gone environmental lately as part of some research he's doing for the Park) and filled two small Tupperware tubs with corn chips. Then an apple each and our Yeti bottles filled from the water cooler; it all went into our soft, reusable lunch coolers.

I set the coolers by the back door and sat down just as Nans was putting the piping hot omelet at my place.

"Perfect timing!" she said, kissing me on the head. "Toast?"

"No, thanks," I said as I dug in. The omelet was delicious—the perfect start to a Monday morning.

"Mmmm. tastes just like fancy restaurant cooking!" I said.

That's a family joke of ours, since we all pitch in at the Park and Nans actually does do a lot of the cooking there. We all say it anytime a family member cooks anything.

Nans swatted at me playfully with a dishtowel and turned back to the counter to clean up.

"Nans," said Skylar though a mouthful of Cocoa Snacks. He was already on his third bowl.

"Yes, my love?" said Nans, scrubbing the frying pan.

"When's it my turn to bring donuts to school for my class? All the kids are asking."

Nans turned off the water and looked at Sky with a smile. "Have you checked the chart?"

Sky shook his head.

Since so many people in the family and in town ask for free donuts all the time, Nans and Grandpa finally had to make a giveaway chart to hang at the Park to keep track of donations.

My aunt Melissa is the accountant at the restaurant and Donut Dreams, and she said we'd fall into financial ruin if we didn't keep better track of our donuts.

"You can't keep giving away all of your product for free to every bingo night in town! Here's the rule: Twice a month. Four dozen at a time. That's all we can afford. Tell people to sign up early," she said.

So that was the rule. Each of the seven grandkids got a turn to bring donuts to school once a year, and we tried to time it to our birthdays. Some families bring cupcakes to school but we bring donuts. People love it.

The best part is that when it's your turn, you get to go into the restaurant really early in the morning and fill the four boxes with the four dozen donuts in the flavors of your choice.

My BFF, Casey, is totally down with this tradition and starts reminding me the week leading up to my birthday how much she **loooooves** our cinnamon donuts.

As if I didn't know that by now. As if I wasn't already slotting a dozen cinnamon donuts into my birthday assortment way in advance!

Nans continued, "Okay, I'll check the donation calendar for you when I get to work and I'll let you know this afternoon. Your birthday is next month, Sky-baby, so it's coming up!"

Sky grinned and some gluey chocolate mush oozed through his teeth.

"Ugh!" I groaned and went to clean up my dishes and get my things for school.

Minutes later, we were in the car and on our way.

❈ ❈ ❈ ❈ ❈

As soon as I walked into school, I saw Casey.

"Hey!" I said, coming up behind her and pulling on one of her long, dark curls.

"Hey, girl!" Casey said, twirling me around and grabbing me in a hug.

"Long time no talk," I joked, since we try to always text right before we go to sleep and right when we wake up.

We're on a Snapstreak right now—haven't missed a day in two weeks—and we're trying to keep it that way. We like setting silly goals like that for ourselves.

"I have a big scoop!" said Casey, her dark eyes wide and her eyebrows scrunched way high in excitement.

But before she could fill me in, we were interrupted.

"What's up, chicas?" asked my cousin Kelsey, popping open her locker.

She's in my grade, as is her sister, my cousin Molly. They aren't twins, which is confusing since they're almost the exact same age.

My aunt and uncle adopted Molly from Korea and then my aunt had a surprise baby, Kelsey. I liked having them both in my grade—they were so different that they each added a lot in different ways—but we all had our own small friend groups.

"Hey, Kels," I said.

I wanted to hear Casey's news, but I wasn't sure if it was for public consumption. I glanced at her and she looked ready to burst.

"Guess what?" Casey said, looking all around the busy hallway. She lowered her voice to a throaty whisper and Kelsey and I leaned in. "We're getting a new student today!"

"A new student? Now?" blurted Kelsey loudly, swiveling her head and generally making a Kelsey-like scene. Kelsey doesn't do anything in a small way.

"Shhh!" said Casey. "My mom will kill me if she thinks I'm spilling news."

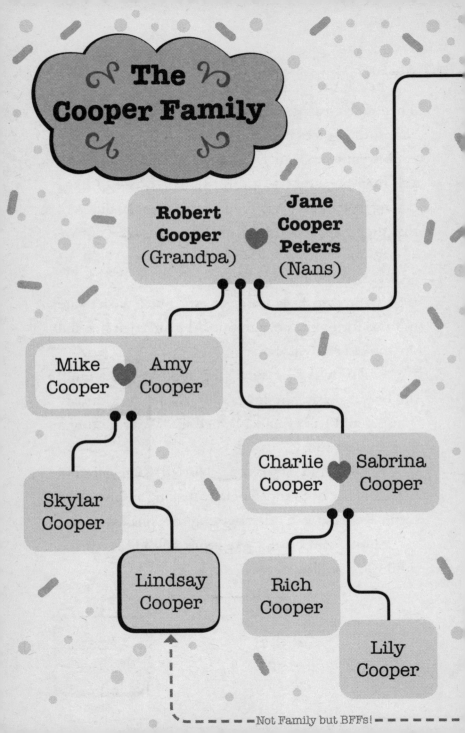

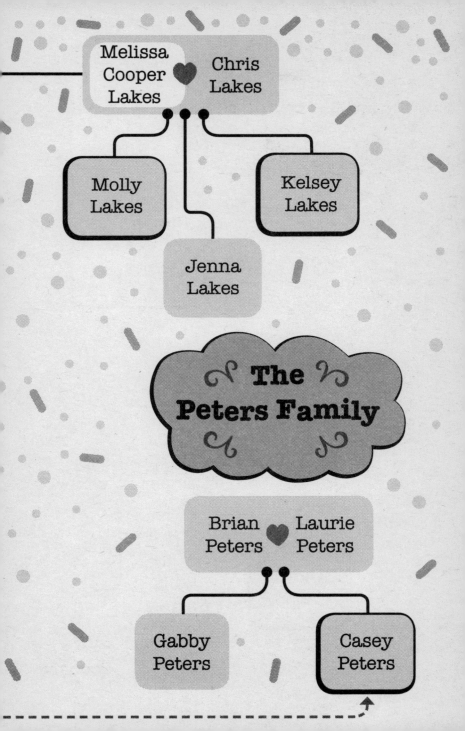